The Fabergé Diamond

A Donald Carter Mystery

John Buchak

Cover Design: Karin Buchak
Photos by www.dreamstime.com

ACKNOWLEDGEMENTS

To my family and friends who for many years have encouraged me to keep writing my novels, thank you.

To my sister who reads my stories and helps me with a first editing and suggestions in my writing, thank you Carol.

To my daughter who listens to my ideas and then puts all of my writing in book form, thank you Karin.

To my friend Rick Rofman, thank you for all your help in reading and editing after my attempts at rewriting.

To P. Chester Daley, wherever he might be.

1

The office of Donald Carter Security and Investigations, Inc. was located on the second floor over a truck repair shop in North Hollywood, California. It was exactly what one might expect if he were looking for a crappy office in a bad neighborhood. Carter, who just never seemed to rise to his true potential, was actually a very good investigator but with many bad habits.

Located at the rear of a lot the size of a football field, the property also included a second building that was occupied by a retail glass shop. The entire property was surrounded by an eight foot chain link fence with a large gate entering from a side street and another from the main boulevard. The two story building was once the truck maintenance facility of the affluent North Hollywood Glass Co. Now the first floor garage area was a business called John's Truck and Auto Repair, and the second floor offices were being rented by a couple of small businesses, one of them Donald Carter Security and the other Trident Exterminators.

Old dark green metal stairs that led to the two businesses on the second floor were attached to the side of the concrete building. They were in desperate need of paint and creaked anytime someone walked up or down them. As customers started their walk up the stairs they couldn't help but see the two brightly painted signs on the wall that were nailed in place along the right handrail. The first read Trident Exterminators. The second, a much smaller sign, read, Carter Security, with an arrow pointing on an angle up the stairs.

At the top of the stairs the gray metal door stood opened outward, tied with a bungee cord to the railing. A rusted bell-shaped light attached to a pipe hung over the doorway. Two large dirty windows, one on each side of the door amazingly gave the dingy looking hallway a small bit of light. An arrow painted on the knotty pine wall pointed to the left that read "Trident." One pointing to the right read only "Security."

The small outer office of Carter Security, behind the half-wood, half-glass door, had one desk and several filing cabinets. The desk, in the center of the room was free of any mess, with only a phone, desk pad and a roll-a-dex phone number holder. A copy machine sat on a small table next to two of the filing cabinets on the left wall. With the exception of the window on the right wall that looked out onto the boulevard in front of the building, all the walls were a dark knotty pine. A door marked 'PRIVATE' was directly behind the desk and normally remained open.

Sitting on an old brown faded and cracked leather couch, Annie Dugan was taking notes that were being dictated by her boss, Donald Carter. Miss Dugan, a young and pretty red-head, had been hired by Carter right after graduation from high school three years earlier, as a favor to her father.

Carter, who sat in his old wooden swivel captain's chair behind an oversized oak desk, looked at the ceiling as he dictated to Annie. His size twelve white sneakered feet were crossed at the ankles and planted on the right side of his otherwise empty desk.

Being a US Army veteran of the Vietnam War and an ex-Los Angeles Police Department Detective, Carter had a very busy few years from graduating from high school to the present day. His enlistment in the service for four years provided him with Military Police experience. Not long after his discharge he attended the Police

Academy and became a patrolman with the LAPD, putting in only eight years with the police force before saying one day, "I've had enough of this shit" and resigning.

With the experience he had gained as an MP and his years with LAPD, he applied for and was granted a Private Investigator's License. On his first paying investigation, he successfully located a thief who had been stealing information from a large computer company and was paid handsomely and gave his company its first bit of recognition in the industry.

On this particular day Carter was dressed in his favorite pair of Wrangler blue jeans, white tee shirt and a Dodger's baseball cap, in anticipation of going to the Dodgers/Giants game that night.

As Annie was returning to the front office, a knock came on the outer door that at first startled her. The door opened and a beautiful tall dark-haired woman walked in.

"Hello Mrs. Wade, Annie said. We weren't expecting you today."

The woman had come into the office without an appointment several days earlier to hire Carter to help locate her brother. With a substantial retainer of one thousand dollars, Carter agreed to look into the disappearance of her brother. Other than checking out an address in Hollywood, he had done very little to earn his fee at that point.

"Is Mr. Carter in? I need to speak with him. It's urgent?"

Hearing what the woman had said, Carter called out while still seated at his desk, "Annie, would you show Mrs. Wade in please?"

As the woman, dressed all in black walked into the private office, Carter stood up and offered his hand, "I'm sorry I haven't gotten back to you Mrs. Wade, but there is nothing new on your brother's disappearance. The lead you gave me on Hillcrest Road in Hollywood turned out to be a dead end."

Still standing, looking more like a construction worker than a private investigator, Carter's 6'2'' frame and 225 pounds of un-sculptured muscle seemed to block the sunlight rays coming in the window behind him.

Although the private office resembled the front office with the knotty pine walls, there was a door on the left side of the room that housed a toilet, sink and medicine cabinet, with an adjoining door to the Trident office next door. The floor of the office was covered with a dark gray commercial type carpet, and the windows had vertical blinds which were open with a view of the two streets.

Even though Carter asked the woman to have a seat, she remained standing and said, "Mr. Carter, I would like you to end the investigation into my brother's disappearance. You may keep the balance of the retainer for your troubles. If there are any additional charges I would like to settle up now."

"You do understand, Mrs. Wade, that you are entitled to my services for another two days?"

"Yes, but I would like you to stop now."

First letting the woman know that there were no additional charges for his services, he then informed her, "If there is anything I can do for you in the future, please don't hesitate to call me."

The woman offered her hand, said thank you and left the office as swiftly as she arrived.

Annie came back into the office and asked, "Close the file on that one?"

Carter said, "I think we might be seeing Mrs. Wade again, possibly in the near future."

Approximately thirty minutes after Mrs. Wade's departure, Annie came into Carter's office and told him, "There's someone on the phone who says he must talk with you immediately."

Picking up the receiver, "Donald Carter here, how can I help you?"

"Mr. Carter, my name is Serge Creshanko. I would like to retain your services to locate someone."

"Mr. Creshanko, I would be very happy to provide you with my services. Please prepare a list starting with the name of the person you wish to locate, a complete description and the reason why you wish this person to be found. I will be in my office tomorrow after 9AM. At that time we can discuss your situation."

"Mr. Carter, I must meet with you today."

"I'm sorry sir, but that's not possible. I have a previous engagement that I must keep. Tomorrow morning is the earliest we can meet."

"Mr. Carter, may I ask what your normal retainer might be for, say, five days work?"

"In most cases sir, my normal fee is two hundred dollars a day, plus expenses."

"Mr. Carter, I am prepared to pay you a retainer up front of three thousand dollars for five days work, plus your expenses. But we must meet today or tonight before midnight."

Carter thought a few seconds and said, "I'm going to put you on hold sir, I'll be back in a minute."

Annie had been standing in the doorway listening to the conversation and said, "It wouldn't be a good idea to put off a paying customer, especially since the rent is overdue already, Mr. Carter."

"He wants to give me a three thousand dollar retainer for a week's work, but we have to meet today."

"Mr. Carter, we do have other bills to pay."

Getting back on the line, Carter said, "Mr. Creshanko, the best I can do is to meet with you here at my office around 10PM tonight. Otherwise it will have to be in the morning."

"Mr. Carter, that will have to do. I will be at your office at 10PM tonight with the information you asked for."

Hanging up the phone, Carter said, "Write that rent check sweetheart, looks like we have a new paying client."

2

Several miles away from Donald Carter's office that afternoon, in the Hollywood hills, two LAPD detectives were waiting for the Los Angeles Medical Examiner to finish his work. Det. Stanley Croft and Det. Ivan Petrovich sat on the fender of their squad car parked in the driveway on Hillcrest Road in Hollywood. Dealing with a long grueling day, the two detectives had been assigned a homicide investigation that was called in by the apartment building manager. The man had reported hearing shots around 11AM that morning. After a first response by two officers in uniform, the homicide detectives were sent to the scene.

Det. Petrovich had only been a detective for three months and like they say in the business, 'The kid was still wet behind the ears.'

Det. Croft, an old crow of a detective with twenty-three years experience, was still trying to get used to his new partner he called kid.

The rookie detective was rambling on about the new Chevy Corvette he intended to buy as soon as they became available at the local dealer.

Det. Croft cut him off in mid sentence as the young detective was describing the new body design, "Enough car crap Kid, try to concentrate on the two dead Russians in the building."

One of the patrol officers, who had been checking around the perimeter of the building, called to Croft, "Hey Detective, I think we got something over here."

Walking to the front porch, Det. Croft asked, "What do you have Harry?"

Pointing to a crumpled-up white object that stood out on the dark soil under the bushes, the officer said, "It looks like a business card that someone recently tossed there, Detective."

Reaching under the thorny rose bushes, Det. Croft, using a broken small branch, brushed the crumpled card closer to himself so he could pick it up by one of its corners with his handkerchief.

Straightening out the wrinkles, the detective read "Donald Carter, Private Investigator." The detective knew the name very well, and the address. It was right in the middle of the industrial section between Lankershim Blvd and Vineland Ave. Croft also knew he would soon be paying Mr. Carter a visit, but for now his attention was centered on two dead men in the building.

The first person to exit the apartment building was the police crime scene photographer, followed by the Medical Examiner, Dr. Arthur Cox. Croft asked, "We all clear Doc?"

The M.E took off his glasses to wipe the lenses and said, "Yeah Croft, I'm done here. The "bag-em and tag-em guys" will be here in a few minutes, along with the Scientific Investigation Division, (SID) and fingerprint team. It's ok to go back in, but you know the drill, put your gloves on and don't touch anything."

Croft said, "Pretty gruesome in there, huh Doc?"

With a slight smile on his face, the M.E. said, "Well Croft, I'm no detective, but it looks like a straight up execution to me. Hands tied behind their backs, bullet in the head. Was no suicide, that's for sure."

Croft asked, "Hey Doc, you got an extra one of those plastic evidence bags? I found something under the bushes that I need to give to the fingerprint guys when they get here."

The M.E., who was quick to answer, said, "You know Croft, you can't get prints off dog crap."

Croft faked a laugh and said, "Very funny Doc."

After handing the detective one of his evidence bags, the M.E. walked to his car without turning around, saying, "See you around Croft. Don't let the stink of this one rub off on ya."

The young detective asked, "What did he mean by that Sarge?"

"You'll find out in due time, Kid. It's just his sense of humor. He's a morbid son of a bitch."

After placing the business card in the plastic bag, Croft said, "Okay kid, let's go in and take a look around."

Entering the building and walking down the hall heading to room #107, Croft asked his young partner, "Can you smell that?"

"Smell what Sarge?"

"Stop for a second. Now close your eyes and tell me what you smell."

"Are you serious?"

"No, I'm joking. Close your damn eyes and tell me what you smell."

The young detective did as he was told. He closed his eyes and tried to pick up the scents in the hallway. After a few seconds he said, "Someone's cooking bacon and maybe toast."

Det. Croft asked, "What else?"

"I definitely smell coffee, and there's something else that smells kind of foul."

"Take a good whiff kid, that foul smell is the one you better remember. Open your eyes and take a few more steps farther down the hall. Take another good whiff and don't forget it. That's the smell of death. They ain't been dead but a few hours and already they're starting to stink up the place."

Walking into the room, the 95 degree temperature outside was already heating up the day. It had to be at least 105 in that room with the windows closed and no AC. The flies were starting to gather on the faces of the two dead men and along with the pools of blood on the hardwood floor, the smell was very strong and pungent.

Croft told his young partner, "Don't touch anything, the fingerprint crew will be here in a little while, then after that we can tear the place apart."

Petrovich asked, "Shouldn't they have been here by now?"

"Yeah, but they got tied up at that bar shooting on Van Nuys Blvd. A bunch of crazy drugged out bikers shot the place up, and a couple of them got taken out by the bartender and his scatter gun."

"What the hell is a scatter gun?"

Croft smiled, "A shotgun kid. From what I heard, he made chopped meat out of one of the bastards. The second one will also need a closed casket funeral."

Looking around the place, Croft noticed that it was pretty empty. Other than a black leather couch, television, small coffee table and a standing pole lamp in the corner, the room looked barren. A closed door to the right appeared to be the door to the bedroom. To the left there was a standing floral partition. Behind it was the kitchen area with a built in stove, a free standing white refrigerator and a wall phone next to it.

Carefully opening the kitchen cabinets, Croft said, "Just as I thought."

Petrovich asked, "What's that Sarge?"

"This apartment was just a meeting place. Cabinets are empty of food and no pots or pans. Hey kid, go get that manager and bring him back here."

A few minutes passed and the detective came back in the room followed by the apartment manager.

Det. Croft asked, "It's Mr. Soulski? Am I saying that correctly?"

With a very heavy Russian accent, the man said, "Dat is Sol*u*ski, detective."

"Sorry Mr. Soluski about mispronouncing your name."

"Dat is okay Detective. Vhat ken I do for you?"

Croft asked, "Well first off, can you give me the names of the two dead men?"

"Da von I recognize is da man who rents from me this apartment. His name is Alex Rubenevich. The other man I do not know."

"How long has Mr. Rubenevich lived here sir?"

The man scratched his chin and said, "Two monts next veek."

"Do you have any other information? Maybe on a lease agreement or application?"

"He rents mont to mont. No lease, no application. He give me trouble, I kick him out."

"Is there anything else you can tell me about the man?"

"He bad man. He had Russian Mafia looking for him. I told him last veek to get out, dat I no vant any trouble."

"How do you know they were Russian Mafia, sir?"

The man smiled and said, "How do you know you step in dog shit. The stink is all around you. Believe me, I know."

Croft said, "Thank you sir, that will be all for now."

After the man had walked half-way down the hallway, Croft said quietly, "Lying bastard."

15

Petrovich asked, "why do you say that Sarge?'

"Fuckin Rooskis, they all lie and stick together. I'll bet he even knows the shooter."

"You do know I'm part Russian, don't you Sarge?"

"Yeah, yeah I know, that's why we're here. Get over here and read this shit on the wall by the phone."

Walking over to the wall phone, Petrovich looked and said, "I don't know what the hell this says, it's written in Russian, I think."

Croft said, "Right, a fine product of the old country you are. We need to get someone over here that can read and write in Rooski. Get on the car phone and get someone over here."

"Hey Sarge, just so you know, I was born in Woodland Hills and so were my parents."

3

At the age of eighteen, just two months after graduating high school, Donald Carter received the letter in the mail that most young men at that age dreaded, a greeting from the president. The war in Vietnam was progressing hot and heavy and the government was sending out draft notices daily. His number came up and he was given a date to report for induction into the US ARMY.

Talking with an older friend who had survived a tour in Vietnam, Carter was told that if he agreed to the draft, he would most definitely be put in the infantry and be on his way to Vietnam before he could blink an eye.

His friend also told him "If you don't mind a little extra time in the service, you could go see an Army Recruiter and make your own choices of what you wanted to do in the army and where you wanted to serve."

Carter told his friend, "I'll think I'll give it a try, I got nothing to lose."

Carter did just as he said he would. He eventually did do a tour in Vietnam but he was a lot better prepared to help him survive there. And because of his training the day finally came when he was safely headed back to the states for reassignment.

Donald Carter and Michael Terratello first met as they sat side by side on a C 130 airplane leaving Vietnam air space in late 1973. Changing planes in Japan, they continued their conversation and their new found friendship all the way to Travis Air Field in northern California. After sharing a seventy-five mile cab ride to the San Francisco Airport, they parted company. Michael was heading east for New Jersey and Donald south to Los Angeles. Both men were looking forward to a nice long leave after spending the past year in what they considered hell.

Thirty days later they met again, as both were assigned to Fort Hood, Texas. Sgt. Donald Carter,

MP and Specialist Five, Michael Terratello, Electronics and Communications Specialist, were assigned to different units at the fort, but stayed in touch just the same. Both knowing that the remainder of their enlistment would be spent at Fort Hood, they started talking about getting a place off base.

Asking around, they soon found out that a house in a nearby town called Gatesville would be available, but the rent was a little more than just the two of them could afford. Another MP, First Lieutenant Dan McKay, quickly became the third person they needed to afford the house rent.

Over the next six months, the three men became close friends sharing expenses and any women who dared to venture through their front door. Mickey T., Donny Boy and Irish Dan, as they became known, were hell raisers in that little town.

Two months before Michael's discharge, Dan McKay informed his other two roommates that he was on orders to go to Vietnam, but he was getting married before he departed. Since he and Donald were MPs and worked together, he asked him to be his best man.

The ceremony was quick with no frills, and two weeks later First Lieutenant Dan McKay was on his way to Vietnam. Donald and Michael stayed at the house until they were both discharged two months later.

Once again the two friends were saying goodbye at the airport and heading in different directions.

Over the next six years, the two men talked occasionally over the phone and even managed to visit one another taking trips on the two coasts. Then one day, Michael broke the news that he was moving to California. By this time his friend Donny Boy had been Officer Donald Carter with the LAPD for more than five years.

One big reason for Michael's move was that he was constantly being approached by his uncle, Vito Terratello, trying to get him to join the family business. The senior Mr. Terratello, who was know as "Don Terratello" to some, happened to be a well connected man in the Sicilian family on the east coast, and there were very few in a higher position.

Michael frequently told his uncle, "Uncle Vito, I love and respect you and I will never forget my heritage, but that is not the path in life I choose to follow."

With a warm embrace, a kiss on the cheek and a handshake, Uncle Vito wished his nephew a sorrowful goodbye. Michael was also told, "If for any reason you should ever need my help, just call and I will do anything in my power to help you."

With a U-Haul trailer, loaded with some of his prize possessions, and hooked to the rear of his old Ford pick-up truck, Michael headed west. Five days later he was registering at a motel in the northern part of the San Fernando Valley, north of Los Angeles.

Within days of arriving in Los Angeles, Michael found employment with an alarm company using his skills that he had worked at and perfected after his discharge from the military. In his off time, Michael worked out at a martial arts studio earning himself a six degree black belt. To earn a few extra bucks, he also taught young students the art of self defense and thought that someday he might have a studio of his own.

Whenever possible, Michael and Donald would get together and reminisce about old times. Soon after applying for and getting his California Guard card and gun permit, Michael quit his job with the alarm company so he could do private security work. As friendship would have it, he occasionally did work for the newly formed Carter Security Company.

The Dodgers/Giants game that Carter was so excited about going to turned out to be a real pitcher's duel. It was a low scoring and fast paced game with the Dodgers winning one to nothing, getting Carter on his way back to his office by 9:15PM.

Arriving early for his appointment with Mr. Creshanko, Carter decided to call his old friend Mick with one last rub of the fact that his Dodgers beat up on the lowly Giants that Mick liked so much.

After a bunch of ribbing and catching up on the past couple of weeks since they last talked, Carter asked, "Hey Mick, how about going out for a few drinks tonight after I wrap up with this new client?"

"Oh you want to rub it in about my Giants some more, huh Donny Boy?"

"No, you know I wouldn't do that. I would never kick a Giants fan when he's down. Tell you what. The drinks are on me. I'll have my scotch and you your ice tea and maybe we'll pick up a couple of bimbos. I'll wait for you at my office, so get here when you can."

"Okay Donny Boy, you're on, but I can't get there probably until eleven. If I can I'll get there earlier. How's that Mr. Big Winner?"

"Sounds good Mick, but if I'm still with the client just wait in the outer office. It won't take long."

"He's due at ten?"

"Yeah, hold on a second Mick, I think I hear him now coming up the metal steps."

When the outer metal door at the top of the steps squeaked like a parakeet chirp, Carter said, "Yeah that's got to be him, got to go."

"Okay Donny Boy, I'll be there as soon as I can, maybe ten-thirty."

4

Pretending to be reading a file on his desk, Carter looked up when he heard, "Mr. Carter, I presume?"

Standing and offering his hand, Carter was face to face with a well-dressed man approximately sixty years old in a very expensive black pin-striped suit. He stood over six feet tall, broad body weighing maybe two hundred and forty pounds, slightly balding but well groomed gray hair around the edges, and smelled of fine flowery cologne.

Holding his hat in his left hand, the man shook hands with Carter and said, "Sir, my name is Serge Creshanko and I believe I have a very profitable endeavor for your agency."

"Please have a seat Mr. Creshanko and tell me what it is that I can do for you."

As the large man sat in the high-backed cushioned chair positioned directly in front of Carter's desk, an even larger man appeared in the office doorway. The man seemed to completely block off the small bit of ceiling light from the front office as he stood there.

Mr. Creshanko turned his head slightly to the left and said, "Mr. Carter, I would like you to meet my chauffer and bodyguard, Victor."

From what Carter could guess, Victor stood somewhere around 6'6" or 6'7" and weighed about three hundred pounds considering the way he filled the doorway. The man dressed all in black looked very intimidating and not someone Carter would ever want to confront, at least not without a large caliber gun.

Mr. Creshanko told the man, "Please Victor, close the door and wait in the outer office while Mr. Carter and I discuss our business. If I should need you, I will call you."

Once Victor did as he was told, Mr. Creshanko took out an envelope from his pocket and removed a sheet of paper and a photograph and handed them to Carter.

Looking at both items, Carter recognized the woman in the photograph, but pretended not to know her. "Sir, what name is she using and do you have her last known residence or where she was last seen?"

"Mr. Carter, I don't want to beat around the bush. Her last known residence that I can confirm was the Beverly Hilton in Beverly Hills. And the last place she was seen was walking down your steps after meeting with you just the other day. You do of course recognize her do you not, Mr. Carter?"

Sitting back in his swivel chair, being very careful not to fall over backwards, Carter said, "Mr. Creshanko, it would be unethical of me to disclose any information about another client. But yes, I do recognize her."

"That is fine Mr. Carter. As I said when I first entered your office, an exchange of your talents and information could be very profitable to you. I do of course require complete honesty on your part. If that is a problem, there are other ways we can communicate. Are you refusing to provide me with the information I require?"

"Mr. Creshanko, I believe our business has concluded. What you are asking of me I can not, and will not do. So Sir, this meeting is over."

"Mr. Carter, what I want from you is any information you may have learned from that woman. I also would like anything you may have learned from the two Russian men you visited two days ago on Hillcrest Road."

Carter stood up and said, "I would like you to leave sir."

"Please sit, Mr. Carter. I am not going anywhere yet, not until we have concluded our business. I have explained what I want from you and you will provide me with that information."

Carter didn't sit, but instead said, "Look pal, I don't give a rat's ass what you want from me. I don't know who the hell you think you are, but I'm telling you, I want you out of my office."

Folding his hands on his lap, Mr. Creshanko said, "I hoped Mr. Carter it would not come to this," then he called out, "Victor, would you come in here please."

When the extra large man opened the office door, he was already unbuttoning his jacket and starting to remove it.

Mr. Creshanko said, "Victor, Mr. Carter is having a hard time remembering answers to my questions. Would you please see if you can help him remember?"

As Victor slowly stepped into the room, he tossed his jacket on the couch and rolled up his sleeves. Mr. Creshanko got up from his chair and moved to one side of the room. With the flick of his hand, Victor flipped the high-back chair to the side and stood directly in front of the desk.

Carter said, "Look Creshanko, if you think Man Mountain here is going to make me change my mind, you're sadly mistaken."

With one of his big paws that he had for hands, Victor grabbed the side of the desk and slid it to the left side of the room like it was made of cardboard. Backing Carter into a corner, he then grabbed him by the front of his tee shirt and pulled him close and said, "You will answer the questions for Mr. Creshanko, now."

As though considering what was being told to him, all quiet fell over the office, and Carter heard the familiar chirp of the outside metal door being opened. With a slight smile starting on his face, Carter said, "Fuck you big man, I ain't answering shit. Now call him off Creshanko."

"But this seems to be the way you prefer it Mr. Carter."

5

Victor saw the smile on his face and slammed Carter into the corner one more time before he heard Mick yell out from behind him, "Hey, you started the party without me. I see you moved the furniture. Can I have the next dance big guy?"

Creshanko waved his hand in a very dismissive way, and said, "Victor remove our intruder."

Victor pushed Carter to the floor, then turned and started walking towards Mick with his arms extended. About three feet from him, Mick threw a lightning fast punch with the power of a sledge hammer, striking Victor in the solar plexus. The big man instantly bent forward grasping his chest trying to gasp for air. With both hands Mick reached up and grabbed Victor by his long black hair pulling his head down further. With amazing speed Mick drove his knee upward smashing the big man's nose and then pushed him backwards onto his backside.

While Mick was giving his demonstration on how a 5'11" one hundred and eighty pound man can take down a giant, Carter had crawled to his desk and unlocked the lower desk drawer and taken out a 9mm Glock and chambered a round.

With the gun pointed at Creshanko, Carter yelled, Call him off now."

Victor, who had started to get up slowly with blood steaming down his face, was told by his boss, "Remain where you are Victor."

As Mick walked to the bathroom door, he asked Carter, "Hey Donny Boy, do I get that next dance now?"

"Hang around Mick, this party is just getting started."

Mick stepped into the bathroom, took a towel off the rack and soaked it in the sink with cold water. Ringing out most of the water, he came out of the bathroom and tossed the towel to Victor saying, "Looks like you're losing a lot of blood from that broken nose big man. Use this. It will help."

Holding the towel to his nose, Victor asked, "Vhat da hell did you hit me vit, little man, a baseball bat?"

Mick smiled, "Nah, just a pillow big man."

Looking at Carter, Mick asked, "You okay Donny Boy?"

"Just fine now Mick. Thanks."

"Are you guys done here Donny Boy?"

"Just give me a few more minutes with his boss. Then you can show them both out Mick."

Looking at the man on the floor, Mick said, "How about you and I go outside big man and let these two finish talking business?"

From his seat on the floor, Victor asked, "Vhat you say Mr. Creshanko?"

"Go Victor. Go out for some fresh air. I'll be fine. Mr. Carter and I have a little more to discus."

Watching the big guy get up from the floor, grabbing his jacket from the couch, Mick said, "Go ahead big man. I'll be right behind you."

Still holding the gun in his hand, Carter asked, "Why do you think I would still have anything to discus with you Creshanko?"

"Mr. Carter, you locate the items I'm looking for and you stand to make $30,000."

"The woman is worth that much to you?" Carter asked.

"Not just the woman Mr. Carter, it's the knowledge she carries."

"So now besides the woman, you want me to locate what?"

"The woman is in possession of information that can lead you to antiques that were stolen many years ago from Russia."

"What kind of antiques?"

"That will be revealed after you locate the woman."

"Bullshit pal, you reveal it now or get the hell out."

"They are jewel incrusted eggs Mr. Carter.

"Eggs, all this shit is over some fucking jewel-covered eggs?"

"That's right Mr. Carter. The jewel covered eggs in question come from a collection that disappeared from Russia over sixty years ago. There were nine missing eggs in all. I am in possession of four of the nine. Two eggs have recently been discovered and returned to Russia. They were of no concern to me. The remaining three that I wish are very plain in design, but are worth a finder's fee of over fifty thousand dollars."

"Wait a minute, you only offered me thirty thousand."

"The woman was given twenty thousand with the understanding she would receive the balance upon delivery."

"And let me guess, she took the money and disappeared?"

"Yes Mr. Carter, I believe she received information, as did you, from the two Russians on Hillcrest road as to the location of the missing eggs, and then she killed them."

Reaching slowly for the inside pocket of his jacket, Creshanko said, "I am only reaching for another envelope Mr. Carter."

"That better be all that comes out in your hand."

Laying the envelope on the desk, Creshanko said, "As I first promised, here is your retainer fee of $3,000.00."

"What makes you think I still want your money? And why the hell should I believe anything that you've told me?"

"You have nothing to lose and much to gain. If you find nothing, you've made the retainer for just that, nothing. But, if you locate the missing eggs, you stand to have a nice pay day in your future."

"How do I get in touch with you Creshanko?"

Handing Carter a card that he wrote a number on the reverse side, he said, "I know you will succeed Mr. Carter. You are very good at what you do. Your reputation has proven that. Call me when you have located the woman, or have new information for me."

As Creshanko turned to leave the office, Carter said, "Get one thing straight Creshanko, I will not turn the woman over to you so you can torture or murder her after you have gotten what you want from her. I will not break the law or do anything illegal. But if I do locate your precious eggs, I will expect payment to be made in cash the way I dictate. Is that understood?"

"It is understood Mr. Carter. I feel that we understand each other completely. Good night."

Hearing Creshanko's footsteps as he walked slowly down the steep metal steps, Carter walked to the outside door and stood on the landing. The black limo that Creshanko arrived in was parked near the bottom of the steps. Victor held the rear door open with one hand, while the other hand still held the towel pressed against his nose.

Carter couldn't hear what was being said, but he saw Creshanko talking with Mick. After a loud laugh, he shook Mick's hand and gave him a card. Once the rear door closed, Mick looked at the card and put it in his shirt pocket.

Watching the limo pull out of the driveway, Carter called out, "Hey Mick, you ready for that drink yet?" Then he walked back inside to his office.

About thirty seconds later Mick walked into the office and sat on the couch and said, "He offered me a job. Do you believe it? That son of a bitch offered me a job working as a personal body guard!"

"And what did you tell him?"

"I told him I would think about it."

Carter plopped in his chair and said, "You what?"

"Hey Donny Boy, you know something, that big ass Victor dude is really a pretty nice guy."

"Hey Mick, have you lost some of your marbles? That fucker would have killed me if you hadn't shown up when you did."

"Nah, I don't think so. Oh sure he would have fucked you up a bit, but kill you, Nah."

"Okay that's it! I'm putting you on the payroll. What do you make an hour when you work for that security outfit?"

"They pay me eight bucks an hour with a two day a week guarantee minimum. Why?"

"Starting tomorrow morning you're on the clock at twelve bucks an hour plus expenses. How's that?"

"Can't do it Donny Boy."

"What do you mean you can't do it, not enough?"

"Nah the money's fine, I'm just busy tomorrow morning, with a private job."

"What kind of private job. Not for that asshole?"

"Nah, for some rich dude who wants me to be his body guard for a trip to the bank. He's got a shitload of bearer bonds and a bunch of cash he needs to bring to his safe deposit box at his bank.

"Okay, how about you meet me here at say, two o'clock in the afternoon and we'll check out the Beverly Hilton Hotel for a woman I need to track down."

"Who's the woman?"

"Long story. Come on, let's check out Rusty's Hacienda and see if we can pick up a couple of those bimbos I was talking about."

"Sorry, got to pass on that tonight Donny Boy, but tomorrow you're on."

"Tomorrow night we'll be working, spending some of that asshole's retainer. Go get your beauty sleep and I'll see you around two tomorrow."

As Mick started to leave, he stopped and said, "You know, they have a dress code at the Hilton, no jeans and tee shirts allowed there."

"Hey, I do have suits and I got a new pair of sneakers."

"Very funny. I'm pretty sure Charlie Brewster is a security guard at the Hilton. He might be able to help us get information."

"Sweet dreams Mick, now get the hell out. If you change your mind, I'll be at Rusty's."

6

Rusty's Hacienda on Lankershim Blvd., has been a mainstay of North Hollywood for many years, serving great authentic Mexican food and the best Margaritas anywhere.

When Carter entered he didn't see anyone other than the bartender that he knew, so he just plopped his butt on a stool and ordered a double shot of Dewars White Label scotch on the rocks.

It was around midnight when a tall good looking blonde walked up behind him and tapped him on the shoulder and said, "You alone handsome? I'm feeling hot and I need someone to share my loving."

Turning on his stool, Carter looked into the woman's eyes and said, "Not anymore sweetheart."

Cindy Prentis was an old time flame of Carter's. He knew right away that he would be getting laid that night when she asked, "How about buying a lady a drink?"

Carter had just finished his second double scotch but when the bartender came over he said, "Hey Paco, how about two of your super-sized Margaritas?"

The bartender, who knew him well, said, "Coming right up Mr. Carter."

Two hours and four Margaritas later, it was 2am and the lights were flashing. The bartender was saying, "Sorry folks, but it's closing time, everybody must go, thank you all for coming."

There was no way Carter could drive, but since Cindy lived only one block away from the bar, it would only be a short stagger around the corner to her house. So the two happy-go-lucky drunks made their way holding on to each other, bumping and stumbling to Cindy's abode.

Once in the house, Cindy mixed two drinks. A few minutes later they found their way into the bedroom. They stumbled along, he pulling her sweater over her head, and she unbuckling the belt of his jeans. Somehow they managed to strip each other clean, falling into bed looking forward to having a great sexual experience.

Getting an erection at first was easy for Carter, but maintaining it, no way. Cindy was hot and wet, Carter was soft and sleepy. With a trip to the kitchen freezer, a handful of ice cubes, a towel and very experienced hands and mouth, Cindy finally got Carter erect and functioning again.

Carter became very aggressively passionate as he used his tongue and fingers to stimulate Cindy's vagina causing her to scream out with each orgasm.

It was approximately 4am when Cindy whispered into Carter's ear, "You were great tonight Carter, and we have to do this again, but there's one little problem. My husband should be getting home in a couple of hours and you can't be here."

Carter sat up and said, "Your husband? When the hell did you get married?"

"You remember Buddy Steele don't you?"

"Yeah, he's doing three to five up in Tehachapi for armed robbery."

"Oh, he got out six months ago and we took a trip to Las Vegas. He was such a sweetheart so we tied the knot."

"But he must have been on parole; he violated parole going to Vegas."

"Oh Carter, it was just a weekend. We were back on Monday so Buddy could go to work. He got a job working downtown loading trucks on the graveyard shift. He gets off at 6am and usually rolls in here around 6:30; that's why you have to go. We can do this again next week, how about that?"

Carter was already stumbling around getting dressed just as fast as he could, "Cindy I don't think that would be a good idea. Don't get me wrong, you are one hell of a woman and a great lay, but I make it a practice not to mess with another man's wife. I hope you understand?"

"I understand just fine Carter. Get what you want, then it's wham bam and time to scram. Don't let the door hit you in the ass on your way out."

Carter couldn't move any faster if he had a rocket up his ass. Making his way to his car parked in the lot at Rusty's, the cold morning air worked like a miracle to help sober him up, at least enough to drive the one mile to his office.

Although still quite drunk, Carter was wise enough not to try to drive the fifteen miles west to his home at the other end of the Valley.

With all the traffic lights in his favor, it took only a few minutes to arrive at the locked gate of the office lot. Another few minutes to pull in, park the car and walk up the steps and he was safe from the eyes of the police. Fumbling with his keys in the dark he finally got the outside door open.

Once inside, Carter walked with the help of the moonlight shining through the windows down the dark hallway. After unlocking the outer office door, he switched on the light pulling the door closed behind him. Studying a clear path to his office, he then turned off the light and carefully made his way to the bathroom to relieve himself, then to the awaiting couch for a little shuteye.

Sitting on the couch, Carter managed to get one sneaker off before he fell sideways and dozed off as soon as his head hit the cushion.

7

Lying on the couch tossing and turning, his dreams were taking him to strange places. With a heavy feeling in his chest, a pounding in his head, and a burning in the pit of his stomach, Carter envisioned himself lost. Looking left then right, he started running down a dark hallway just as fast as he could, knowing he couldn't let up one bit. The hallway had no windows or doors and seemed endless. Suddenly, a flashing lighted sign appeared in the distance on a wall that read, "Coffee Bean Plantation straight ahead." Trying to run faster towards the lights, he could now smell the strong scent of the coffee beans and then he heard a man's voice faintly ask, "Hey Carter, you take it black or with all that crap in it? Come on, I haven't got all day."

Rustling around finally realizing that he had been dreaming, his hand felt the dried out leather of the couch beneath him. Slowly opening his eyes he saw he was facing the back cushion of the couch. Once again he heard, "So Carter, you want it black or with all that crap in it like a sissy-boy?"

Identifying the voice, Carter asked, "What the hell do you want Croft?"

"For now, you can tell me if you want any crap in your coffee?"

Rolling over facing the room and seeing the face of the old detective, Carter said, "No, black is fine Croft, thanks."

"Come on Carter, don't you have a warm greeting for your ex-partner?"

"We were partners for only seventeen months Croft. You hated my guts and I hated yours, case closed. Now what the hell do you want?"

"Hey, but it was a learning experience for you. Being a young detective and all, you had a lot to learn."

"Ok, enough with the walk down memory lane Croft, what the hell do you want? I got a pounding in my head that just won't quit, so get to it."

"You want it sugar coated and you want me to beat around the bush, or do you want it right between the eyes, no holds barred?"

"Get on with it Croft will ya."

"Ok Kiddo. What was your business with the two Rooski's over on Hillcrest Road?"

"What makes you think I even know what the hell you're talking about?"

"Come on Carter, you think you can bullshit me. I know you were there, so why were you there? "

"Well then tell me what you got Croft? You know, right between the eyes, my head just isn't clear enough for all this chess playing you're doing."

Det. Croft pulled the plastic bag out of his pocket with the crumpled card in it and held it up so Carter could see what it was. Then he said, "It's a homicide investigation Carter, so stop with the bullshit."

"Okay Croft, here's what I can tell you without violating a confidence. I was trying to locate a client's brother and the last place he was seen was at that address. When I got there, I rang the bell and a couple minutes later this guy answers and asks me in broken English, "What do you want?" "I told him who I was looking for and he said, 'Never heard of him,' and then he closed the door. So I knocked real hard and he opens up again, and I say, "Look, in case you hear from him call me," and I handed him my card. He looks at the card, crumbles it up and throws it in the bushes and says, "Fuck off," and slams the door shut."

"That's it Carter, nothing else?"

"That's it."

"Okay, so who is the client?"

"You know better than that Croft, I don't have to reveal who my client is. You and I both know that you can't make me divulge that information."

"It's a homicide investigation Carter. There are no loopholes you can use. So open up and maybe we can avoid going to Police Headquarters to continue this conversation."

"You think you can threaten it out of me then give it your best shot Croft."

"Hey you're right, I can't argue that. Now here's what I can do. I can get one of those judges downtown to sign a warrant for me. Then I can come back here with a crew and go through all your files because my investigation involves a homicide, and you are holding back important information. I may not find anything, but you'll have one hell of a mess to straighten out."

"What kind of bullshit is that?"

"No bullshit Carter, it's a double homicide investigation, which gives me a lot of extra clout."

Appearing not to know what the detective was talking about, Carter said, "Homicide, whose homicide?"

"Oh, did I forget to mention that both of those Rooski's were found real dead. Yeah, with their hands tied behind their backs and a couple of 22's placed carefully in the back of their skulls?"

"Yeah Croft, you kind of left that part out."

"So who was the client Carter?"

"Well since she's no longer a client, her name is Patricia Wade, and she's disappeared."

As Croft wrote the name in a small notebook, he asked, "What about an address and phone number?"

"No address and the phone number she gave me was for Ling Toys Chinese Restaurant down on Melrose. I checked it out myself. I think the name was phony also, but she paid in cash."

"Okay Carter, that's it for now, but if you hear anything from her, I need you to contact me, ASAP. Oh, by the way, I like what you've done with the office, but you need to clean up that blood over by the door. To me, I don't care. But you don't want other people asking too many questions. Take care Carter; we'll be talking again real soon. If I were you, I'd lay off the booze. It seems to be kicking your ass."

"Yeah, thanks for the advice. I'll consider it. So long Croft."

Annie Dugan, who had been in the outer office, came into Carter's office and said, "I'm so sorry Mr. Carter, he was waiting on the steps when I arrived this morning."

"Its okay sweetheart, actually talking with him helps me in *my* investigation."

"Does that mean I can still mail the rent check after I make a deposit this morning?"

Carter walked to his desk and opened the top drawer and took out the envelope that still contained $2800.00. He removed $800.00 and gave Annie two grand and said, "Deposit this sweetheart. There's enough there for the rent and fifteen hundred extra."

"I'll pay a couple of the other small bills and keep the rest in reserve in case we fall on hard times."

"There should be more to follow if everything works out right in the next few days. Listen, I need to go home and take a shower and get back here to meet Mick at 2pm so we can go to the Beverly Hilton to question someone. Close up the office, go to the bank, and then get back here and take care of whatever comes up."

"Okay Mr. Carter, don't worry, I'll take care of everything."

"If Mick should call, tell him we're still on for two o'clock. Anyone else calls, just get all their information and I'll call them back."

8

Carter arrived back at his office at 1:30, spotted Mick's 1960 Black Cadillac convertible parked in the lot and quickly went up to his office. Walking into the office he found Annie sitting behind his desk and Mick seated on the couch. Mick was dressed in a pair of black pants, a light blue shirt, black tie and a black blazer. Carter was wearing dark brown slacks, a tan shirt, dark brown tie and a brown and tan herringbone sports jacket. Both men were dressed appropriately for the trip to the Beverly Hilton.

Mick smiled and said, "Hey Donny Boy! I never saw you look better. Where did you get the duds?"

"Mick, you should see some of the shit I have hanging in my closet, you wouldn't believe it."

Laughing loudly Carter added, "Hell I don't believe it."

"Hey Donny Boy, I made a call and found out that the guy I know is on duty there this afternoon. I did some work for him about two years ago and he's now the Chief of Security at the Hilton."

"That could come in handy Mick. Do you know if he'll talk with us about one of the guests?"

"Hey, it's a shot in the dark, maybe we'll get lucky."

Carter asked Annie, "Sweetheart, were you able to get to the bank to make that deposit?"

"I sure did Mr. Carter, I wrote a couple of checks that need your signature."

After signing three checks, Carter said, "Annie, the third check is for you, a little back pay."

"Thank Mr. Carter."

Carter said, "One more thing Annie. Please type up a retainer receipt for that guy Creshanko for the three thousand. I'll call him when I get back to the office if I decide for sure to take his case."

"Okay Mick, you ready to go?"

"Let's do it Donny Boy, we're going there in style, that's why I brought my rag-top."

"Aren't you worried about those valet parking guys scratching up your baby?"

"Hell no boss, I'm really fond of my Caddy, but they got more insurance than that old buggy is worth. Come on, let's get going."

The drive to the Beverly Hilton took only a half hour and when Mick pulled up to the valet parking, the attendant had a big smile on his face as Mick handed him his keys. He got the valet parking ticket and said, "Try not to bang it up too much, it's a classic."

The Beverly Hilton was one of the grand old hotels in Beverly Hills. It was first opened in 1955 by Conrad Hilton, one of the richest men of the time. The extravagant interior included a bar lounge named Trader Vic's that was one of the most exotic in all of Beverly Hills.

Before sitting on a stool, Carter looked around and saw only a hand full of people who appeared to be sipping drinks and talking at the far end of the bar. A young couple was seated at a table in the corner looking like they wanted to be left alone. One other customer was standing with a drink in his hand watching as people strolled by the bar entrance. Carter waved the bartender over after he and Mick were seated.

The bartender introduced himself, "Hello gentlemen. My name is Jimmy, what can I get you?"

Mick spoke up and said, "Hello Jimmy, I'd like a tonic with a slice of lime please."

The bartender looked at Mick as if he had just been insulted. Mick told him, "Don't worry Jimmy, my friend here will make up for me. Tell him what you want Donny Boy."

Looking at Mick first, before turning to the bartender, Carter said, "Jimmy, I'll have a double shot of Dewars on the rocks and start a tab for me please."

The bartender asked, "And what room are you in sir?"

"We're not guests here Jimmy, we're just visiting."

"I'm sorry sir, I can't start a tab for you if you're not a guest here."

Carter pulled out his wallet and removed two one- hundred dollar bills and placed them on the bar and said, "Just print out the tab and if you must, take it out as we drink."

After pouring the drinks, Jimmy brought a printed tab over and placed it under the hundred dollar bills and said, "I'll total it up when you're ready to leave sir."

Carter said, "Thank you Jimmy."

After looking around the room, Mick asked the bartender, "Jimmy, can you tell me where Charlie Waters might be today?"

"I'm sorry sir, but do you mean our Chief of Security?"

"Yes Jimmy, that's who I mean."

"I believe he's out by the pool, sir, with the assistant manager. Would you like me to ring him for you?"

"No that's okay. I'll just walk out to the pool. I know the way."

Carter asked, "What do you have in mind Mick?"

"I think I'll just go out there and strut around and show off my fancy duds. I'll be right back. Why don't you and Jimmy here get to know each other a little better, maybe show him that photograph of the woman."

Carter took out the picture of Patricia Wade and asked, "Hey Jimmy, you ever see this woman here in the bar?"

Looking only briefly at the picture Jimmy said, "I'm sorry sir. I can't discuss anything about our guests at the hotel."

"Whoa Jimmy, we're not discussing anything about her yet. I just want to know if you have ever seen her in here."

"I'm sorry sir, I can't give you any information about one of our guests."

"So you're admitting to me that she is or was a guest here at the hotel?"

"Sir would you like another drink? That is something I can help you with."

From behind, Carter heard, "Hey Donny Boy, I'd like to introduce you to someone."

Turning on his stool, Carter noticed a very tall muscular man in a perfectly tailored black suit.

Mick said, "Charlie Waters, I'd like you to meet my boss Donald Carter of Carter Private Security."

The two men shook hands and Charlie Waters asked, "So, what can I do for you Mr. Carter?"

"Well first thing Charlie, you can call me Don. Did Mick fill you in any on what we're working on?"

"He told me you're looking for a woman who stayed here at the hotel for a few days. Can I see that picture you have?"

Looking at the picture Charlie said, "She's a real looker. I remember her." Then he called out, "Hey Jimmy, you remember this one don't you?"

Jimmy walked over from the other end of the bar and said to Charlie, "Can we talk in private please?"

A couple of minutes passed and both men walked back and Jimmy said, "Look, all I can tell you is that she was a guest at the hotel up until a few days ago. From what I know, she had paid her bill and checked out. She came back into the bar two nights ago and had a couple of drinks down at the end of the bar with some gentleman."

"That's it, Jimmy?"

"I can't say anymore sir. I could lose my job for what I have just told you."

Charlie said, "I have to get back to the assistant manager, I hope I was of help. Nice meeting you Don. Mick, drop by again when you're in the neighborhood."

All three men shook hands and Charlie left the bar.

Carter had an idea and asked, "Hey Jimmy, you ever play any bar games?"

Jimmy said, "I've been known to play a few sir."

"Ok let's start with this." Carter took one of the hundred dollar bills and asked Jimmy, "Would you break this into five twenties please?"

Laying the twenties out on the bar next to each other, Carter then said, "Okay Jimmy here's what we do. For every question I ask you that you don't answer I take a bill away. For every question you do answer I put a bill back. Whatever is left when the questions are done, belongs to you for a tip."

Jimmy said, "Forget about it sir! I told you I can't answer any more of your questions."

"Hey Jimmy, what have you got to lose? Come on, give it a try. Here's the first question. Can you tell me if the woman was alone when she came back in the other night?"

"No sir, I can't tell you anything more."

Carter took a bill away and the said, "Okay that's one for me. Did she happen to mention if she would be back?"

"I'm sorry sir but I can't help you."

Carter took another bill away and asked, "Did the woman appear to be waiting for someone?"

"Again, I can't help you."

Carter took another bill away and asked Mick over his shoulder, "Hey Mick, do you think one of the maids around here could use an extra hundred to answer a few questions?"

Before Mick could answer, Jimmy said, "She was here with a short heavyset bald guy."

Carter smiled and put one of the twenties back on the bar and asked, "You didn't happen to hear what they were talking about, did you Jimmy?"

"They were speaking in some foreign language; I think it might have been Russian."

Carter put another bill back on the bar and asked, "Did you happen to hear anything that might help us locate her?"

Jimmy smiled and gently took the remaining bill out of Carter's hand and said, "I heard them talking about Russian restaurants that were all located in the Valley and West Los Angeles."

Carter asked, "Anything else Jimmy?"

"It looks like you're out of bills sir."

Carter picked up the other one hundred dollar bill and said, "For this, you'll have to tell me where she moved to."

Jimmy smiled and said, "I heard them talking about the Sportsmen's Lodge in Studio City."

Handing the hundred to him, Carter said, "You've been a great help Jimmy. Take the drinks out of this, and keep the change. Thank you."

9

The Sportsmen's Lodge and Hotel has a long history in the San Fernando Valley. Sportsmen's Lodge, as it was called when first opened in the 1880's, was built around an underground artesian spring that fed the lake. The valley at the time was sparsely populated and the lake was an oasis for travelers. In 1910 the name of the lodge was changed to "Hollywood Trout Farms," but in 1945 it was renamed Sportsmen's Lodge.

Movie stars like Clark Cable, Humphrey Bogart, Lauren Bacall, Betty Davis, John Wayne and Roy Rogers spent many nights at the lodge. John Wayne in his early film career was known to fish in the pond at the lodge and have the cooks prepare the fish for his breakfast. Robert Kennedy stayed at the lodge the night before his assassination.

When Mick drove down Ventura Blvd. and attempted to pull in to the parking lot at Sportsmen's Lodge, he was stopped by an LAPD car blocking the driveway. Driving onto the next driveway, it also was blocked by a patrol car.

Carter told Mick, "Pull into the gas station on the corner Mick and let me out. I'll go find out what's going on."

Carter walked from the gas station to the first patrol car and recognized the officer immediately as one he remembered from his days wearing the blue uniform. The officer couldn't tell him much but he did say, "A call came in that the cleaning lady found a stiff in one of the rooms when she went to do her clean up job."

"Who's working the investigation Gary?"

"Croft is back there with Lieutenant Kester and the crime scene crew."

"Thanks Gary, I need to ask the hotel manager a few questions. Is there any problem with me going in to talk with him?"

"Hey you know the drill Carter, no one in, no one out."

"Ok Gary, but Croft is going to be pissed when he finds out I was here and you didn't tell him."

"Does he know you're coming?"

"He told me he wanted to talk with me again, ASAP. I have information about a woman he's looking for in his homicide investigation."

Officer Gary Tridel told his partner, "Officer Bellows, keep an eye on things, I'm going to take him back to see the sergeant."

Carter said, "Do me a favor Gary. Let's go through the office so I can ask the manager a question. The answer from him is something Croft will want to know when we talk."

"Carter, if you get my ass in trouble with Croft……"

"Don't worry Gary, like I said, Croft wants to see me."

Walking in the front door, Carter spotted a couple of well dressed men behind the hotel check-in counter and assumed one of them might be the manager in charge.

Spotting the tag on his jacket that read, "MANAGER", Carter approached him and asked, "Excuse gentlemen. May I have a word you sir?"

The manager motioned to the man standing next to him and said, "Burton, would you handle this please?"

Carter said, "My question is for both you gentlemen. I only need a minute of your time."

The manager said, "What is it sir, we're very busy around here at this time."

Carter took out the picture of Patricia Wade and asked, "Sir, have you ever seen this woman? Is she or was she a guest at this hotel."

The manager looked quickly at the photograph and said, "Sir, I think you should be talking with the detective in charge of the investigation. It's taking place in one of our rooms in the rear of the buildings."

"So you do recognize her sir?"

The Manager looked at the officer standing by Carter's side and said, "Officer, I believe you need to escort this gentleman to the back to talk with your superior. Now good day." The man then walked away.

Carter thanked him as he walked off and then started walking with the officer. The walk through the hotel and back out to the side parking lot only took a minute, and a couple more minutes to reach the rear of the building. During that time the manager must have notified Sergeant Croft, because he was rounding the corner of the rear building and walking towards Carter and the officer.

When they were finally face to face the sergeant asked, "What the hell are you doing here Carter? And you Officer Tridel, why are you escorting this man onto a crime scene?"

Before the officer could answer, Carter said, "That's my fault Croft, I told him I had information for you on Patricia Wade, and that you wanted to talk with me, ASAP."

Sergeant Croft said, "Return to your post Officer Tridel. Carter, you come with me."

The slow walk back to the rear building took a couple minutes because the two men kept stopping every few steps as Carter started to explain about the Beverly Hilton.

Rounding the corner it was easy to see which room was being worked in. Approaching the doorway Sergeant Croft was met by one of the SID techs who handed him a plastic bag containing a business card. The sergeant looked at the card and then asked Carter, "So what can you tell me about this, Carter."

Looking at the card, he saw it was one of his and said, "She must have taken a few cards off my desk Croft."

Sergeant Croft asked, "She? Who said it's a woman in there?"

Carter looked into the doorway and saw a fairly heavy-set white baldheaded man lying on the bed. He was dressed only in boxer shorts and a massive amount of blood on the pillow could be seen under his head.

The sergeant asked, "Another one of your satisfied customers Carter?"

"I don't know him, never saw him before Croft."

From inside the room someone said, "That's Sergeant Croft, Mr. Carter. Show some respect please!"

Lieutenant Dwayne Kester slowly walked out from inside the room and said, "Nice to see you again Don. Now, what are you doing here?"

Lt. Kester and Carter were old friends going back to high school days. Dwayne went on to college while Carter joined the army and both men met again at the police academy years later.

"Offering his hand, Carter said, "Hello Dwayne, how have you been?"

Holding up both his rubber gloved hands, the lieutenant said, "I'll tell you what Don, we'll have coffee later and catch up, but for now, what the hell are you doing here?"

"Well, in some little way I think I'm connected to your victim in there."

After taking the plastic bag from Sgt. Croft and holding it up, the lieutenant said, "I think you're more than just a little connected."

Carter said, "I don't know how he got one of my cards, because I never gave it to him, I've never seen him before."

Lt. Kester said, "He probably got it from the woman who was staying in the room next door."

Sgt. Croft spoke up and said, "The Wade woman, Carter."

Lt. Kester said, "Thank you Sgt. Croft, but I'll deal with Mr. Carter."

The lieutenant and Carter walked out into the parking lot away from everyone to find a quiet place to talk. Removing his gloves and taking out a cigarette, the lieutenant asked, "So what's your take on all this Don? What's the story on this Patricia Wade?"

Carter filled in his old friend on everything he knew about Patricia Wade, leaving out only the thing that concerned active paying clients like Serge Creshanko.

What Carter found out was that Patricia Wade had stayed in the room next to the dead man. Mrs. Wade had last been seen by the assistant manager at 9am that morning checking out of the hotel.

The dead man had no identification, no wallet and no passport, nothing to explain who he was. The name used when he checked in was John Dumont and he used cash as a deposit and payment for his room.

Finishing his conversation with Kester and promising to call him if he remembered anything else about the Wade woman, Carter walked to the hotel front lobby. Mick was seated in the lobby having a cup of coffee as Carter walked in and called out, "Hey Donny Boy, how about a coffee and croissant?"

Only slowing his pace a little, Carter said, "Let's get the hell out of here Mick, we got a lot to do."

Mick smiled, "Where to next boss?"

"We need to check out a few Russian restaurants and bars. Do you know of any off hand?"

"There's only one I can think of, and it's in Studio City or North Hollywood."

"Let's head back to the office first Mick, and I'll look up a few more Russian places to check out."

"Well boss, at least we're dressed for it."

10

Of the six restaurants that specialized in Russian cuisine in the yellow pages, two were in the San Fernando Valley and one was on Melrose in West Los Angeles. The other three were located between twenty to thirty miles away. The first three were listed as authentic Russian food.

The Moscow Grotto in Glendale was off the beaten path. It was located in a commercial area, far from the shopping malls and heavy flow of pedestrian traffic. So when Carter and Mick searched it out they were a little leery of the location.

Still dressed in their fine duds and looking like two tourists out on the town, Mick parked his Caddy in the lot next to the building. The parking lot, on the left of the building, had only six cars parked more to the rear of the property. Mick was able to park close to the front of the building, but he still put up the roof, and set the alarm.

The front of the building had a sidewalk entrance with a lit-up sign above two big red doors. A large mural was painted on both of the windows to each side of the front door depicting scenes from Russian cities.

Walking through the front door, Carter knew immediately that this was not a restaurant that a classy lady like Patricia Wade would be dining in.

The interior of the restaurant/ bar was in such disrepair, obviously in some stage of remodeling with no signs of any food being served. The three men seated at the bar, who had been talking loudly in Russian when Carter and Mick walked in, immediately silenced themselves and just stared at the fancily dressed intruders.

Carter thought to himself, 'What the hell, we're here, I'll show them the picture and we'll be on our way.'

Approaching the men, Carter held out the picture of Patricia Wade and asked, "Sorry to intrude gentlemen, but by chance have either one of you ever seen this woman before?"

The three men just stared at him and said something in Russian and then the bartender came over and asked, "What is it sir that you are trying to find out?"

Carter held up the picture and said, "I was just asking these gentlemen if they had ever seen this woman before."

The bartender laughed and said, "Sir, unless you asked them in Russian, they wouldn't understand you. Let me have a better look at that picture."

The man put on a pair of glasses and said, "I don't believe I have ever seen this woman before."

Cater thanked the man and looked at Mick and said, "Let's go Mick. We have another stop to make."

The drive to the Red Square Restaurant in West Los Angeles took only a half-hour from Glendale, so Carter and Mick got there just after 8pm. The problem was parking on Melrose Blvd. The closest parking space they could find was two blocks away and Mick was not very happy about leaving his car that far away from the restaurant, even with his top of the line alarm system.

As they walked through the front door of the restaurant, all eyes seemed to be on the two men and a hush fell throughout. Carter was approached by a man dressed in some type of costume with a red vest over a white shirt and a turban with a fez on it dangling to one side.

The man spoke in broken English and asked Carter and Mick, "This is a private party gentlemen. Can I help you in some way please?"

Carter said, "I'm sorry sir, we didn't mean to intrude on your party, but we thought this was a restaurant that was open to the public."

The man said, "It used to be, but now it's only for private parties, weddings and special meetings."

Carter excused himself and he and Mick walked the two blocks back to the car. On the way, Carter said, "That's strike two, Mick. We'll try one more and then call it quits for the night."

Sitting in the car before starting the engine, Mick asked, "Where to next, comrade?"

Carter smiled and said, "Very funny Mick. Let's head back to North Hollywood to that place off Laurel Canyon. I've heard about that place before, great food, music and a completely authentic ambience, it's called The Bolshoi Village."

The first two Russian restaurants they visited were total shit-holes compared to The Bolshoi Village. Just looking at the front of the building, the guys knew this place had class.

Not wanting to use the valet parking, Mick circled the block three times with Carter complaining in his ear before someone pulled his or her car out of a parking space very close to the building.

The building was in a strip mall but the restaurant took up four of the six stores. As they walked on the cement walk leading to the front entrance, they could hear music coming from the open windows and door.

Walking through the doorway, they were met by a man dressed in a very expensive looking suit who asked, "Good evening gentlemen, do you have a reservation?"

Carter said, "Good evening, no I'm sorry we don't have a reservation. Would it be possible for us to sit at the bar please?"

"I'm sorry sir, but all admission is by reservation only."

Carter took out his money clip and removed a twenty dollar bill and placed it in the man's front jacket pocket and asked, "Could you check your reservation list again?"

Once again the man said, "I'm sorry sir but...."

Carter removed a hundred dollar bill and made sure the man saw it and placed it in his pocket. The man said, "Let me look again sir. Ah yes, we just had an opening. Do you gentlemen mind sitting near the kitchen door?"

Carter said, "That would be fine. And what is your name please?"

"My name is Ira sir, I am the maître d'. If you would just wait here for a minute, I will make sure your table is prepared."

A couple minutes went by and Ira came back to where Carter and Mick were standing.

"Ira said, "Gentlemen, your table is ready. Would you follow me please?"

The table looked as if it had just been placed and set next to the busy kitchen doorway. Once seated, a waiter quickly provided the men with menus and a wine list. Waving off the wine list, Carter ordered a double Dewars on the rocks and a tonic with a slice of lime for Mick.

The Bolshoi Village was actually a very large establishment, much larger than it appeared from the outside. With the inner connecting walls removed, the restaurant was quite oversized for such a small complex. Looking over the large number of diners dancing or seated at their tables, Carter also could see several open doorways that led to private dining rooms he assumed.

The soft sounds of dinner music were coming from a quartet of musicians who were performing on a raised stage in the far left corner of the restaurant.

Both Carter and Mick ordered the same meal of stuffed cabbage, potato pancakes, string beans and a small cup of red beet borscht as an appetizer.

After completing the wonderful dining experience and being entertained with fine music, Carter once again studied his surroundings carefully. As he pointed out different murals on the walls to Mick, he noticed that they were being watched by several men positioned around the restaurant.

When Carter caught the eye of Ira, he waved him over and showed him the photo of Patricia Wade and asked, "Ira, by any chance have you seen this woman in here at any time? She may have been in the company of a much older Russian gentleman?"

Ira studied the photo for a few seconds and said, "I'm sorry sir, but I don't recognize this woman at all."

As Ira started to hand the photo back, Carter asked, "Perhaps by chance your bartender might recognize her."

Carter watched as Ira walked to the end of the bar and signaled the bartender over and showed him the photo. The man looked up quickly appearing startled, said something to Ira then walked away.

Returning to the table, Ira said, "Philip does not know the woman and has never seen her before."

Taking the photo back, Carter said, "Well Ira, it's been a wonderful evening, the food was delicious, the music entertaining and meeting you a pleasure. If you would bring me the check please, we will be on our way."

Leaving enough cash along with a substantial tip, Carter and Mick got up from the table and calmly left the restaurant, falling in behind a slow walking party of three men and one woman who had first blocked the door buttoning their coats then walked out ahead of them. Halfway down the cement walkway, the group stopped walking and blocked the path of the two men again.

First excusing themselves, Carter and Mick stepped around the group and each suddenly felt a hard object pressed against their backs and were told, "No sudden moves gentlemen, if you both just do what you are told, no one will be harmed."

A couple who had been talking at the end of the walkway disappeared quickly and Carter was told to walk ahead slowly, while Mick was told to stay where he was.

As Carter was led around the corner of the building, a black stretch limo slowly pulled up and the rear door was opened by a man walking next to the car. From inside the limo a man's deep voice said, "Good evening Mr. Carter, would you please get in and have a seat."

Carter hesitated and the man said, "Don't worry about your companion. He will be released unharmed as soon as we drive away. I promise you that."

As Mick watched, the stretch limo pulled away and just as the man had told Carter, he was released unharmed and told to be on his way. The man also said, "Your friend will be released unharmed after his conversation. He will be delivered to any destination he chooses."

With not much of a choice, Mick walked to his car and sat there for several minutes before starting his Caddy and driving back to Carter's office to wait.

11

The man seated in the far corner of the back seat of the limo, illuminated only by the dim interior light of the vehicle, listened as Carter spouted off about being kidnapped and the laws about such actions. Finally with a slight laugh in his voice, the man said, "Enough Mr. Carter, you're not being kidnapped. We are just going for a little ride to have a private discussion."

"Having a gun pushed into my back and ordered into the back seat of an unknown vehicle constitutes kidnapping according to the law."

"Please Mr. Carter let's not beat around the bush. I want you to know that my intentions and methods sometimes are misunderstood. I apologize if I have offended you, but you will be amply rewarded in time. Now to business, please. You have been passing around a photograph of a woman that I am also interested in locating. Tell me sir, what is your interest in this woman?"

Carter leaned forward in his seat and said, "First off, you're going to tell me who the hell you are before I answer any of your questions."

The man laughed and said, "You are not in control of this conversation Mr. Carter. It is my questions that are to be answered, not yours."

"Look buddy, you want anything from me, you're going to tell me whom I'm dealing with. I'm not in the habit of negotiating with people who put a gun in my back and then refuse to tell me who they are. That's my terms."

"Mr. Carter, don't be foolish, with just a word from me I can have a drug administered to you and you will tell me all that I need to know. Is that what I must do to have you cooperate?"

"If that's how you want to play it pal, you better go for it, because you'll get nothing from me voluntarily."

Laughing again, the man said, "The information I have received on you was very accurate, and I'm sure that you will not disappoint me. Very well Mr. Donald Carter, you may call me Boris and that is how you will always refer to me. You will not reveal that name to anyone for any reason."

Now it was Carter who laughed and said, "Boris? You mean like Boris and Natasha from the Rocky and Bullwinkle kids show, how fitting?"

The man laughed again even harder and said, "Your sense of humor is wonderful, Mr. Carter. Yes, like the children's TV show. Now enough of your fooling around. The woman please, what is your interest in her and what information have you been able to gather about her?"

The man Boris, who sat across from Carter, turned on an overhead light and removed a cigar from a compartment in the seat in front of him. The bright light gave Carter his first good look at his interrogator. Boris had a round face with the top of his head as slick as a cue ball, clean shaven and a slightly red complexion. The elegant pin-striped black suit he wore appeared first rate, obviously custom tailored and very expensive. Even the scent of his cologne had the essence of class. The name Boris fit him well, as if he had been selected from Central Casting to portray a high level Russian diplomat.

Carter lit a cigarette and said, "Boris, It would be unethical for me to reveal my interest in the woman, if she were still one of my clients. But since she is no longer a client, I could be swayed if I knew what your interest in her was."

Laughing again, Boris said, "You amuse me Mr. Carter. Very well, my interest is in the knowledge that the woman carries in that beautiful head of hers. I believe she knows the location of certain artifacts that were stolen many years ago from my government."

Carter said, "The eggs?"

"Yes Mr. Carter, the eggs, the jewel covered eggs. What do you know of them?"

"I know that you're not the only one who has an interest in locating the eggs or the woman."

Boris smiled and said, "Yes Creshanko. I know of his desire to locate the eggs, and that it is for personal gains of wealth and power. My interest is solely to return them to my homeland and the people of Russia."

"Boris, because Mr. Creshanko is soon to be a client of mine, I can not legally divulge any information about our conversations or of my intended commitment to him."

"Very honorable Mr. Carter, but I could care less about Creshanko. He is an evil man who will be dealt with at another time. My interest is in the woman, her safety and where she can be found."

"Well in that case Boris, we are both at a dead end. It seems a trail of death follows that woman, so the police have a great interest in her also."

"I'm aware of that Mr. Carter. For that reason I have to conduct my business in complete secrecy."

"So what is it you want from me Boris? Do you want to retain my services? It may be a conflict of interest?"

Boris took a puff on his cigar and said, "In a manner of speaking, yes. If and when you locate the woman, I want to be informed. After that you can then go back to your business if you so choose. For this you will be paid a handsome finder's fee. You may decide to stay in my employ and follow this search to the end. Know this Mr. Carter. I do not intend to harm the woman in any way only to question her and possibly offer her protection from Creshanko. It is very important that I find her before he does."

"What the hell is it about the damn eggs that make them worth killing people? Why is there an involvement with the Russian police and Russian Mafia? You're not the KGB, are you Boris?"

"Let's just say, Mr. Carter, that the value of *these* Fabregé Eggs is greater than anyone would ever expect."

"So they're Fabergé Eggs? But how much could they be worth? One million? Five million? How much value do you put on human life?"

"The value Mr. Carter is greater than money. They were the prize possessions of the Russian Tsar Nicholas II, his wife Alexandra and his mother Empress Maria before the revolution. There were fifty eggs created by Peter Carl

Fabergé, a young master jeweler who was appointed 'Goldsmith to the Imperial Crown.' From what is known, only forty-two have survived, and some of those are in private collections around the world.

"Seven very special eggs were redesigned by an unknown jeweler just before the Tsar and his family were removed from their home, hidden away and then executed. All the eggs were incrusted with diamonds, rubies and other gems. All the eggs were stolen after the death of the Tsar. Some of those original eggs that are in the hands of the private collectors cannot be purchased for any price but they are documented. Most of the eggs are in a museum in Russia, but those other seven have not resurfaced until lately. It is rumored that Creshanko has four of the seven in his possession, but it can not be proven until he exposes them."

Carter lit another cigarette and said, "So, there's some fancy eggs out there somewhere that people are killing each other over. And you want me to believe that you just want to bring them home to Mother Russia, with no financial gain for yourself. Is that correct Boris?"

"That is correct Mr. Carter, and this *will* be accomplished with your help."

Boris removed a billfold from his inside jacket pocket and took out a business card. After writing something on the back of the card he handed it to

Carter, "Call me Mr. Carter, when you have located the woman. The number on the front is the Russian Embassy in New York. When you call you ask for extension seven one seven. You will get a recording. Just say 'Carter' and the number you can be reached at, nothing more, and I will return your call. The number I have written on the back of the card is my car phone. You may try that first if you wish, but in most cases it is better to call the embassy."

"Okay Boris, I will expect at least the same amount for a retainer that I received from Creshanko."

Laughter was followed by, "In time Mr. Carter, in time."

Without Carter realizing it, the driver of the limo had traveled along the freeway and turned around and headed back to North Hollywood. As they pulled up to the driveway by Carter's office, Boris said, "I'll be expecting your call Mr. Carter. Stay safe and beware of Creshanko, he is a very dangerous man."

Getting out of the limo and closing the door, Carter noticed Mick's Caddy parked by the office steps. Mick was sitting there watching as the car drove off.

Watching the limo pull away, Carter thought to memorize the license plate, but there was none.

Mick walked over to him and asked, "So where the hell have you been Donny Boy?"

Carter smiled and said, "Getting an education Mick! Getting an education!"

"So who was that guy in the big black car, Donny Boy?"

"Believe it or not, the guy's name is Boris, another Russian looking for that woman and some damn jewel-covered eggs."

"Where do we go from here boss?"

"You can take off Mick, and as soon as I get something from my office, I'm calling it a night and heading home. I'll meet you for breakfast at Lal's Diner at 8am sharp."

Carter watched as Mick drove off and then climbed the stairs to his office. After unlocking the outside door and walking in, he was struck by a blow from out of the dark knocking him completely unconscious.

12

When Carter started to regain consciousness and slowly opened his eyes, he had a hard time focusing on the sliver of light shining under the door in front of him. Lying on the floor on his side, with his hands and feet tied together, he found it very hard to move. Blinking his eyes several times trying to focus on that small bit of light, he remembered being struck with something and then he felt the pain as his head throbbed.

Quickly realizing that he could not break free from his restraints, Carter yelled out, "Okay, I'm awake; now what the hell do you want?"

A few minutes passed when he heard footsteps walking towards the door. Then with a loud, "clack" the door was unlocked and opened. When the light in the room was turned on, Carter quickly closed his eyes from the blinding glare.

Serge Creshanko stood in the doorway while two of his men lifted Carter off the floor and sat him on a folding chair.

"Hello Mr. Carter. It's so nice to see you again, only this time we will talk and it will be with me having the upper hand."

"Are you out of your fucking mind Creshanko? Don't you know kidnapping is against the law, you asshole?"

"Mr. Carter, such vulgarity. I am still your client, am I not? Consider this Mr. Carter, If I am no longer your client, what need do I have of you" I advise you to think before you answer."

"You want my answer? Untie me, Creshanko."

"Foolish I am not Mr. Carter. Answer my question?"

"You are still my client Creshanko; now get these fucking ropes off of me."

With a wave of his hand, Creshanko said, "Untie him Vladie."

Rubbing the back of his head once his hands were free and feeling a large bump but no blood, Carter asked, "Now what the hell is this all about?"

"Mr. Carter, you have been talking with many people in the past few days and I insist on a complete report on everything you have uncovered."

"If you would have shown a little patience, you would have received a phone call from me in the morning. My intent was to have you come into the office and sign a contract and give you a receipt for your retainer. At that time I would have provided you with my initial report."

"So tell me now Mr. Carter, what have you found out about the woman?"

"What would you like to know first? I tracked the woman to the Beverly Hilton just to find that she was long gone? Through some heavy interrogation, I found out that her next stay was at the Sportsmen's Lodge in the Valley. It was cut short and a dead man was left in her wake. I'm in the middle of my investigation, so let me do my job. When I have something else for you, I will let you know."

"Do you think I'm a fool Mr. Carter? Do you think I know nothing of your meeting with Boris Segura? My eyes and ears are out there in the community everywhere. I know where you go and whom you talk with. Now, I need to know what Segura told you and then I have to decide what to do with you."

"What the hell are you talking about Creshanko? He questioned me and I questioned him. I told him nothing and the little bits and pieces I picked up from him are just a start. That Russian mobster knows less than either of us, he asked the same questions I have been asking. Something I am sure of though, a call from Patricia Wade any day now. My assistant is making arrangements to help us locate not only the woman but also those Fabregé Eggs you seek. Once I locate the woman and those damn eggs, I will expect the balance you promised her. How's that Creshanko?"

"Mr. Carter, I want you to know that your life means nothing to me, but because of your willingness to cooperate with me and locate the antiques I desire, you will live to see another day. But know this, if I find that you have tried in anyway to deceive me, I will not hesitate to snuff you out like a burned out candle. Is that clear?"

"Fine Creshanko, now what you can do for me is have one of your stooges get me a few aspirins and some scotch. Then what I will require from you is an additional $3000.00. These days it costs an awful lot to bribe people to open up and talk in this town. It seems your Russian comrades are very reluctant to talk to anyone other than you."

Creshanko laughed and said, "Vladie, get the man the drink and aspirins, also the money he wishes from the safe. If you'll excuse me Mr. Carter, I must make an important phone call in the next room. I will come to see you in your office when you call and inform me that you have more information for me."

As Carter sat with his head throbbing and taking in his surroundings while waiting for his aspirins and scotch, he tried to figure out what his next move might be.

Creshanko returned at the same time as his man with the things Carter had asked for. Swallowing three aspirins and washing them down with a big swig of scotch, Carter asked, "What now Creshanko, does your man drive me to my office, or do I have to call a cab?"

"Now Mr. Carter, you will sleep. When you awaken you will be in the comfort of your office."

Carter looked first at the aspirin bottle then the bottle of scotch and said, "You son-of-a-bitch," and tried to stand only to fall back in his chair with the room spinning around. Within seconds, he closed his eyes and his head fell forward.

True to his words, Carter had been returned to his office in North Hollywood and placed on his couch.

The smell of brewing coffee was strong and as he opened his eyes and started to roll over, he heard, "Well good morning Donny Boy. Had a rough night, did you? You decide to go out for a few drinks after I left?"

"Oh shut the hell up and get me a cup of coffee will ya Mick. While you're at it, get me the aspirins in the medicine cabinet."

"A bit touchy this morning I see."

"What time is it Mick?"

"Well I got 8:45am, but I could be off."

"How long have you been here?"

"About fifteen minutes."

"How the hell did you get in?"

"Well let's see. The outside door was unlocked and your front office door was wide open. Let's just say I walked right in. What the hell did you do after they dropped you off last night?"

"I walked into my office and I was slugged on the head and taken to see Creshanko by a couple of his stooges. When I woke up, I was hog tied and questioned. I guess he liked my answers because I'm still alive. I'm going to get that bastard, Mick, and he isn't going to see it coming."

"Two kidnappings in one night. That woman must have some real important info that they want?"

"Yeah, she seems to be the only one who knows the location of those eggs."

"So what's the plan Donny Boy?"

"I'm going to need your Uncle Vito to do me a favor Mick. You told me you just talked to him the other day when he called and he asked about me during your conversation."

"I would think real hard before you ask my uncle for help. In my uncle's world it is better to do favors for him and not the other way around.

It's not that he wouldn't help. It's what he's going to want in return for a favor some day."

"That's why I'm going to have you ask him Mick. He wouldn't turn down his favorite nephew, or ask for much in return."

"Okay Donny Boy, what is it that you want from my uncle that you're ready to sell your soul to *me* for?"

"I know your Uncle Vito is big in the art and antique collecting world. And I suspect he knows all kinds of people with information about some rare antiques. I need all the information he can get on Serge Creshanko, Boris Segura and the Fabergé jewel-incrusted eggs that seem so important and very valuable. Next, I need to know what it will take to bring that son-of-a-bitch Creshanko down. Also, I need to know where that bastard lives."

"And what is it that you have to offer him for these favors, because he will ask?"

"Mick all I can offer him is my loyalty, friendship and cooperation in any future legal dealings he might have out here on the west coast. And there is always the possibility of a shit load of money if we happen to locate those damn eggs."

"Okay boss, make up your list of what you want, including the names of the people you want information on. I'll see what Uncle Vito can do for you. Just remember old buddy, asking a Mafia Don for a favor can be hazardous to your health."

Carter wrote down a few names and as much information that he knew on each and handed the list to Mick.

"Okay Donny Boy, I'll see what I can find out from Uncle Vito. It will probably take a couple of days though."

"I'll tell you what Mick, take a few days off and call me when you get something. I need some healing time anyway. I'm going to hang around here and wait for Annie and catch up on whatever she has dealt with while we've been running around."

Taking off his jacket, Carter felt something in the inside pocket. Pulling out an envelope he said, "Would you look at this. I told that son-of-a-bitch I needed more money, and I'll be damned if he didn't give it to me. I just hope it isn't counterfeit."

"That's good, mister money bags, because I could sure use a few bucks in advance on my pay."

Opening the envelope, Carter counted out $3000.00 and handed Mick $500.00 of it saying, "Consider this a week's pay Mick. Close the doors on your way out, okay."

13

Carter had lain back down on the couch and was dozing off when he heard the radio in the front office go on and Annie Dugan singing, "I can't get no/ sat-tis-faction/ I can't get no/ sat-tis-faction," as she drowned out Mick Jagger and the Rolling Stones on the radio.

Opening the door to the inner office and walking in with a handful of mail, still singing, Annie was startled when she heard Carter say, "Sounds like you're ready to go on the road sweetheart."

"Oh I'm so sorry Mr. Carter. I didn't know you were here yet. I didn't notice your car in the lot."

Carter sat up slowly and said, "Just putting in a little overtime Annie. So what's been happening around here that I need to know about?"

"Mr. Carter, you really need to call that Det. Croft. He has called here three times and said if you don't call him today he's going to get a judge to type up a warrant for your arrest."

"I'll call him Annie. What else ya got?"

"You got a call from some guy named Charlie Waters who left a number for you to call him back."

"Did he mention what he wanted?"

"Nope, just said that you would know what it was about."

"Anyone else Annie?"

"Yep, that Patricia Wade called yesterday."

Very excited, Carter asked, "What did she say? Where is she? Did she leave a number to call her back?"

"She didn't leave her number but she said she would call you back this morning."

"Did she tell you where she was staying?"

"No she didn't, but she said it was very important and that she'll talk to you as soon as possible."

"Shit, I really need to talk with her Annie, it is very important. I was going to head on home to shower and change out of these clothes but that's out now. I'm going to call that detective and cool his ass down. If Miss Wade calls, let me know immediately okay?"

"Yes sir. There was one other call where someone left a message on the answer machine the other morning around 3am. I'll set it up so you can hear it after you call that detective. There are about ten other messages on the machine that are just bull. Those I'll skip over."

"Annie, would you please get that detective on the phone while I splash some cold water on my face and take a few aspirins?"

"Sure Mr. Carter, I'll get him."

Carter stood slouched over the sink in the bathroom when he heard Annie say, "Det. Croft is on the line Mr. Carter."

Picking up the receiver even before he sat down at the desk, Carter said, "Hello Croft, what is it that you want now?"

"That's Det. Croft to you Carter."

"Yeah, yeah, and that's Mr. Carter to you asshole. Now what the hell do you want, before I hang up on your ass?"

"You do it Carter and you'll be in a lock-up before your head stops spinning."

"Okay detective, enough of the male bonding. What can I do for you?"

"We got another dead Rooski, and guess what he had, your name and phone number on him."

"One of my cards?"

"Actually it was written down in a notebook he had in his vest pocket."

"So who the hell is he?"

"His name is Victor Yeltsin. According to the Medical Examiner he's around six foot eight, maybe three hundred pounds and had his tongue cut out and stuck in his pocket."

"Where did you find him?"

"Off the Golden State Freeway down by the L.A. River in Griffith Park. Oh, one other thing, he had two bullet holes in the back of his head. Sound familiar?"

Carter said, "That big dumb bastard. Yeah I know who he is or was. He worked for a client of mine, a guy named Serge Creshanko."

"How do you know him Carter?"

"Like I said, Creshanko is a client and he was accompanied by the big guy when I first met him. That's about all I can tell you, his boss is still a client Croft, even though I despise the son of a bitch."

"Where can I find him Carter?"

"All I have is his name. You'll have to find out the rest on your own."

"Maybe I should just bring you in and wait until you open up with a little more information?"

"You'll just be wasting your time Croft. I have no idea where he is."

"If I find out you're lying Carter, I'll burn your ass."

"I'll make a deal with you Croft. I find out anymore on him, I'll call you. You find out something, you call me."

"You know it don't work that way Carter."

"Fine Croft, good hunting!" Then he hung up the phone.

Annie came back into the office and said, "Mr. Carter, the guy that left the message the other morning was some guy named Victor. Do you know him?"

Carter sat back in his desk chair and said, "I did Annie, and he won't be calling back."

"Why is that, Mr. Carter?"

"Because Annie, someone decided he was better off dead."

14

Sitting and listening to the message from Victor, Carter knew he could not hold back this information from Det. Croft.

Carter rewound the tape and asked Annie to get the small tape recorder from the file cabinet and make a copy of the message as he replayed it.

Seeing Carter nod his head, Annie started the tape recorder and they both listened as the answer machine played. "Mee-ster Carter, this is Victor. I vood like to meet with you to discus the deaths of several people that Mee-ster Creshanko is trying to frame me for. I did not kill anyone, but he wants to blame them on me and let the police take me and lock me up. I know I am big strong man, but I kill no one Mee-ster Carter. He is not a good man. I fight for him, I protect him, I lie for him, but I no kill for him. I will call you again and you can tell me where we can meet. You must help me and I help you. Goodbye."

"Sweetheart, you wanna get Det. Croft back on the line. I got to take a leak, let me know when you got him."

As Carter was still dribbling into the toilet bowl, Annie knocked on the door and said, "You wanna take it in there or should I tell him to hold on until you're finished holding on?"

Carter laughed to himself, "Very funny *Miss Dugan*. Please tell the detective I'll be with him in one minute. Thank you."

Walking out of the bathroom shaking his hands after a quick rinse in the sink, Carter asked, "Annie, do we have any paper towels. The damn dispenser is empty?"

"You'll have to use your shirt for now Mr. Carter, there's none left in the closet."

Hands still wet, Carter picked up the phone and said, "Croft, I got something for you."

After a short sarcastic laugh the detective said, "That was quick Carter. Come to your senses, did you?"

"Oh screw you Croft, you want what I have or should I just hang up and let you go on your dumbass way?"

"What do you have Carter?"

"Your latest stiff left a message on my answer machine a couple days ago. It's something you need to hear. I haven't been around here too much so this was my first opportunity to check the phone messages."

"I'd like that tape Carter."

"Relax I made a copy for you. Stop by my office when you get a chance and talk to my secretary and she'll give it to you, I need to get my ass home and clean up. Call me later Croft and tell me what you think after hearing the tape."

"Hey Carter. Thanks."

Hanging up the phone Carter called out to Annie, "Sweetheart, Det. Croft will be stopping by to pick up the copy of that tape."

Annie walked in and asked, "You heading home now Mr. C.?"

"Yeah, I need a hot shower and a fresh change of clothes. If Mick calls, tell him to call me at home. Anyone else, you handle it."

"How about that Wade woman? You want me to just take down her information too?"

"Oh shit! No. If she calls, put her on hold and call me on the second line and I'll decide how to handle it then."

"Okay Mr. C. I'll take care of everything around here."

15

Carter's rental house in Chatsworth, located about fifteen miles west of North Hollywood, sat in a quiet rural area of the San Fernando Valley. Normally the drive home on the freeways took only fifteen or twenty minutes, but on this morning the traffic was backed up and just barely moving. Because of a traffic accident involving a tractor trailer that jack-knifed and was blocking all the lanes on the Ventura Freeway, it took Carter almost an hour to get home.

Listening to jazz on the radio made the trip a little more bearable and helped take his mind off the traffic. The down side of not paying enough attention to what was going on around him was not seeing a vehicle that had been following him from the time he left his office. An old green Ford Pinto had been behind him since he entered onto the freeway in North Hollywood.

Carter first caught sight of and started paying attention to the Pinto when he exited the freeway at the Topanga Canyon exit. He didn't think much of it until they both turned left on Lassen Street.

The Pinto reduced speed and stayed well behind and when Carter pulled into his driveway, the little green car with the darkened windows drove by slowly.

Acting as if he hadn't noticed the car following him, Carter entered his house through the front door. Watching from behind the curtain at a front window, he saw the car make a U-turn and slowly drive past the house a second time and then turn and park on the side street. Walking straight through the house to his bedroom, he then unlocked the desk drawer and removed his 9mm Glock Automatic and chambered a round.

Walking quickly out onto his patio, Carter positioned himself where he could watch both sides of the house in the rear of the yard behind his tool shed.

His wait was a short one, with only a few minutes passing when he heard the side gate to the yard creak as it opened. Entering the yard slowly, a person in a hooded sweatshirt and sun glasses approached the patio door holding a gun and looked in.

Sliding the screen door open the person stepped one foot in when Carter said loudly, "You take one more step into that doorway and I'll put a bullet in the back of your head. Step back slowly and place the gun on the table next to the door. Place both hands on your head. Try anything else and you're dead. Now move!"

Slowly the person stepped backwards, placed the gun on the table as instructed and put both hands on his head. Speaking up, the person said, "Mr. Carter, we need to talk."

Surprisingly, the voice was that of a woman and Carter asked, "Mrs. Wade?"

"Yes Mr. Carter, but the name is not Wade, it's really Regina Volasko, and may I now turn around and lower my hands?"

"Yes Miss Volasko, but slowly, and don't attempt to pick up the gun. You have a lot of explaining to do, lady, and if I don't like what you have to say, I'll be calling the police. Now slowly step inside please."

Not taking any chances after she stepped through the patio doorway, Carter picked up her gun from the table and put it in his waste-band. Before telling her to sit, Carter searched the woman for any other weapons and then they both went to the kitchen table where they could sit and talk.

Carter said, "You can start explaining while I make coffee, would you like some?"

"Yes, thank you."

Taking the time to put coffee grounds into the coffee maker, Carter said, "Miss Volasko, your last name sounds very familiar to me. Why is that?"

"My sister Connie was married to an old friend of yours, Dan McKay."

Carter stopped what he was doing and turned to face her, spilling some water on the counter. "What? You're Dan's sister in law?"

"I believe, Mr. Carter, you served with him in the military many years ago."

"Yeah that's true, but I don't remember you being at the ceremony Miss Volasko."

"As you know Mr. Carter, that wedding was put together at the last minute before Dan's deployment to Vietnam. At the time I knew nothing about it. If I had I would have stopped her from marrying that bastard."

"Bastard? Lady, you have a lot of explaining to do."

"Mr. Carter, since I last saw you at your office, I have talked with my sister and she told me she was worried for her life. Her husband, your old friend Dan, had been tracked down, tortured and murdered last month."

"Murdered? Danny murdered? By who?"

"Connie believes they were Russian assassins, and so do I."

"Does this have something to do with those goddamn eggs?"

"It has everything to do with those eggs because that's exactly what this is all about. McKay stole them while he was in the service, hid them and never revealed where they were hidden."

"Okay Miss Volasko, tell me how the hell he came to be in possession of those eggs. I want to know exactly how and why he stole them, and what your part is in all of this."

"I don't know all of it. All I do know is he did have them and he hid them away for safe keeping until he could find a buyer. At some point he contacted some Russians who expressed a strong interest in the eggs and were ready to pay a large finders fee. He was eventually tracked down by some of those people he had contacted and was murdered before he could disclose where he had hidden them. Now my sister is worried that they will come after her, thinking that she knows where they are hidden."

"And why did you come to me Miss Volasko?"

"McKay told my sister that if she ever needed help, she could trust you and she passed that on to me."

"Just for your information Miss Volasko, you have exposed me to being kidnapped, beaten and questioned by some vicious people. The police have been questioning me about several murders that they have tied me to, and I have a bunch of Russian maniacs following me around. Give me one good reason why I shouldn't just turn you over to the LAPD and wash my hands of you?"

"You were friends with McKay and my sister. Isn't that enough?"

Rather than answering, Carter asked, "What does the name Creshanko mean to you?"

"Somehow he found out about me, possibly from the people I had been questioning the past month. He sent someone to talk with me when I was staying in Beverley Hills at the hotel. We had a meeting and he paid me to locate those eggs, and when I didn't he threatened to kill me. I persuaded him to give me more time, but every lead I came up with wound up a "dead end." I found out about the two Russians in the Hollywood Hills who were murdered after I had talked with them and decided to try to cover my tracks. I've been ducking Creshanko and his men ever since."

"Welcome to my world lady."

"My sister's life is in danger now. I need to get her to a safe place. I had nothing to do with those murders Mr. Carter."

"Bullshit lady! You are more involved with those murders than you realize. I guess you forgot all about that bald little man at The Sportsmen's Lodge. The Police found your fingerprints all over his room. Hell, do you deny having a room next to him and being seen with him?"

"I already told you, he was one of Creshanko's people that were watching me. I didn't kill him. When I saw him lying on the bed I took off because I knew that I might be next. Please you have to believe me, I didn't do it, there are other people out there looking for those eggs that will stop at nothing. Do you have any idea how much those eggs are worth Mr. Carter?"

"For my first guess I'd say more than a buck fifty, but no one has actually filled me in. They seem to be worth more than life itself. Where is your sister now Miss Volasko, and please, no more lying?"

"I'm not lying. She has been staying with a friend in Palmdale. Connie and Dan lived on a small farm in Lancaster. She left her home last week after she found her house was broken into and everything tossed around. It was obvious that someone was searching for something. She knew it had to be those damn eggs. Whoever it was tore the house apart."

"Okay, I need to get cleaned up and get a couple hours sleep. But first I need to get you out of my house. You have so many people looking for you and if you could find out where I live my guess is your trackers are not far behind. Is that car yours?"

"No it's rented."

Where did you rent it?"

"I rented it from Rent-a-Wreck."

"It looks it. And how did you pay?"

"Cash deposit."

"You had to show them your license right?"

"I have a fake ID and license."

"I need to make a call and find a place for you to stay for a couple of days until I check out some things. Sit tight, I'll be right back. Just for the hell of it, what are those damn eggs worth?"

"I don't know for sure, but I've heard it was way up there in the millions."

"Carter looked surprised, "each one or all of them?"

"From what I've heard Mr. Carter, the special ones Creshanko is looking for are worth one hundred million for some reason."

Walking into his bedroom to make a call to Mick, Carter sat at his desk and called the number. Just after the second ring he heard a strange clicking and when Mick picked up after ring number four, Carter said, "Mick its Don. Don't say anything, just listen. You need to meet me at Pappy's location just as quickly as possible. It's very important. Don't ask questions now, I'll explain when I see you. You got that Mick, Pappy's location, just answer yes or no. And Mick, keep an eye in your rear view mirror. You may have company."

Mick just answered, "Yes, I got it straight, see you soon."

John 'Pappy' Burke was an ex LAPD detective who had befriended both Carter and Mick while Carter was still on the police force. Pappy, as he was referred to by his close friends, had died in an auto accident around three years earlier and was buried in the Oakwood Cemetery. It would take Carter only minutes to get to the grave site. Mick living farther away, it would take about fifteen minutes. With only one entrance into the cemetery it would be easy to see if either was being followed.

Foregoing his shower and little nap, Carter walked back to the kitchen and found Miss Volasko sipping on her coffee and eating crackers.

She looked at him and said, "If I don't eat something soon I'm going to pass out. With all that's been going on, I haven't taken time to eat."

He said, "We need to get you out of here now; eating can come later. I'm going to make arrangements with a friend of mine to guard you and hide you out while I play decoy for a while. I have a feeling my phone it tapped, but as long as we can get out of here right away, we'll be safe."

"Do you trust this person Mr. Carter?"

Looking at her gun before handing it back to her, Carter said, "With my life, Miss Volasko."

She said, "Yeah, but what about my life, Mr. Carter?"

Carter looked at her, "Hey lady, you can leave now if you want, or you can trust me. That's your two choices."

"Okay, I'll go with you to meet your friend, but get this straight. I need a hamburger and it better be soon."

Carter stared at her, "How the hell do I get mixed up with these nut cases. Let's go."

16

The cemetery was located at the end of Lassen Street only a few minutes from Carter's front door. Just in case someone had followed the woman, he decided to drive back out to Topanga Canyon Blvd. and travel around a little and take a different route to the cemetery entrance.

Once they entered the Oakwood Cemetery main gate and drove to the grave site, it was easy to spot anyone who might have been following them. Parking in front of the old church on the hill, Carter and Miss Volasko with a clear view of the entrance sat and watched for Mick's car. Ten minutes had gone by and Carter said, "Tell me anything more that you know about the death of the Irishman."

"I'm sorry Mr. Carter, I really don't know any more about what happened to him, all I know is what I told you. When you meet my sister she will give you all the facts about his death."

A few more minutes went by and Carter said, "Here he comes, I can spot that big ass Caddy from a mile away."

Watching Mick drive around the different sections of the cemetery before parking, Carter knew he was just being careful.

Carter and Miss Volasko walked over to the Caddy and got in so they could all have a nice talk and decide what the next move should be.

Carter introduced Miss Volasko to Mick saying, "Mick, this is Regina Volasko, formally Patricia Wade. You remember me telling you about her, don't you?"

"With all due respect Donny Boy, are you out of your mind? This lady is poison. She smells more of death than the hills outside the car."

"Hey, screw you buddy."

Carter said, "Mick, her sister was married to the Irishman. Dan is dead. He was killed by some Russians looking for those fucking eggs."

"Why doesn't that surprise me? Like I said, this woman brings death everywhere she goes."

Regina Volasko shouted out, "Fuck you, what do you know, you asshole."

"Hear that Donny Boy, nothing but class."

Carter said, "Enough you two. Mick I need you to take care of Miss Volasko while I go to Palmdale and Lancaster for a couple of days."

Regina Volasko said, "I'm not staying with him. We go together to my sister's or no one goes! Do you understand that Mr. Carter?"

Before Carter could answer, Mick said, "We need to talk in private boss. You need to know more about those eggs before you go on your egg hunt."

"It's okay Mick, she knows all about those eggs. Go ahead and tell me what you got."

Mick pulled out a small notebook and started with, "Do you have any idea how much those eggs are worth?"

Carter said, "Actually I think I do. With all the crap that's going on, my ballpark guess is somewhere between five million to ten million a piece. Am I close?"

Mick laughed and said, "Not only are you not in the ballpark, but you're not in the same state. The word on the New York streets of the people who know, it's somewhere between one hundred million and two hundred and fifty million for all seven eggs."

Carter said, "What! Are you sure?"

"Hey boss, my uncle doesn't make mistakes when it comes to that many zeros. Get this. There's a sheik in Saudi Arabia who is worth billions from all his oil fields, and he is offering a cool two hundred and fifty million for the complete set of seven. No questions asked about how they are obtained. The money would be deposited in an offshore account in the Cayman Islands."

"So what the hell makes these eggs so special? I've heard about Fabergé Eggs being expensive, but not that expensive."

"I guess there was a document that was hand written by the Tsar himself. It surfaced many years after his death and described these seven special eggs. With all the turmoil in Russia that was leading up to the revolution and eventual overthrow of the Tsar, he decided to hide away a small portion of his wealth. Choosing seven of the most common looking eggs in his family's collection, they were delivered by a trusted messenger along with his most prized diamond to a jeweler for some reconstruction work. The seven sealed eggs were cut open and filled with jewels and resealed exactly the way they originally looked and returned to his wife's collection. Those seven disappeared after the Tsar's execution and never resurfaced until ten or twelve years ago."

The diamond in one of the eggs is rumored to be a flawless yellow diamond, cut to a pear shape and is the size of an extra large chicken egg. The actual carats are unknown, but its estimated value is somewhere around one hundred and fifty million dollars by itself."

"That explains a lot Mick."

"Here's the catch. The diamond is inside one of the eggs. The other six have an exact same size piece of quartz and not jewels, and they all weigh the same. Only the one with the diamond has a special marking that is coded in some way."

"You're just full of information Mick."

"Well here's a little more info for ya. Serge Creshanko at last count has four of the eggs. The three remaining eggs were in the hands of a North Vietnamese general when his private staff car was attacked by a bunch of marauders just outside of Hanoi ten years ago. The general and all his men were killed in the attack. It was later found out that the marauders were American GI's. Our old buddy, Irish Dan McKay was one of the attackers."

Miss Volasko sat quietly with a slight smile on her face and Carter noticed it in his peripheral vision but said nothing.

Carter asked, "Are you sure about this Mick?"

"I learned a long time ago, I don't question Uncle Vito. You want to hear the rest?"

"Talk on, old man."

Mick went on, "Around five years ago two men who had served with McKay in Vietnam turned up dead with their throats cut and the Irishman disappeared. The eggs never surfaced and it was believed they were hidden by him somewhere up north. About a month ago the Irishman's body was found in an oil well field in a place called Oildale. He had been severely beaten and several of his body parts had been cut off. The eggs still haven't been found according to sources in the know."

"Well Mick, we are going on a little trip up to Palmdale to talk with the Irishman's widow. Maybe with the help of Miss Volasko we'll see what she knows about where he might have hidden those eggs."

"Seriously now boss, I think this is one you should walk away from before it's too late. The people who are involved in the hunt for those eggs don't play games; they just kill people who get in their way."

"Mick, I won't order you to come with me, there is no way I'm going to push our friendship to that point."

Regina Volasko spoke up, "You mean us Mr. Carter. We go together or not at all, remember?"

Mick looked at the woman, then at Carter, "Okay boss, I think I need my head examined, but at least with me there watching your back, maybe you won't get a bullet in it. And you, Miss Volasko, if there is any bullshit or tricks on your part I want you to understand something. You try anything that doesn't look kosher, and I'll put a bullet in your head quicker than you can blink. Do we understand each other?"

"Yes, you psychopath, I understand. I want you both to remember something. One day you're going to regret not trusting me."

Carter asked, "Is that a threat Miss Volasko?"

With a smirk, "No, just remember I said it."

Looking at her with a stare, Carter said, "I happened to notice that little smirk on your face before. If you have anything else you want to say, say it now."

"Mr. Carter, your friend here seems to have an uncle who is very knowledgeable about those eggs. You might want to ask him about Creshanko and how we can steer him in a different direction."

Mick said, "How about we find a place to eat and I'll fill you in over some Sushi?"

Carter looked at Miss Volasko, "How about we make that burgers and fries Mick?"

17

Using his new car phone as Mick filled up at a gas station on Topanga Canyon Blvd, Carter called Annie Dugan at the office and said, "Sweetheart it's me, don't ask any questions just listen."

Annie said, "But Mr. Carter."

"Please Annie, don't say anything just listen. Whatever it is sweetheart, you handle it the best you can. I have to leave town but I'll be back in a couple of days."

"But Mr. Carter, I need to talk with you."

"Not now Annie, just use your best judgment."

"The police have been here Mr. Carter."

"Fine, when I come back I'll take care of it. I'll be back in a couple of days, goodbye."

Ending the phone call, Carter felt bad that he couldn't tell Annie anymore about what was going on. He knew it was the best way to handle it and he didn't want her to worry. Not telling her anymore than he did, there was no way she could be found guilty of lying to the police if questioned. Carter knew his suspicions of the phone in his office being bugged would just make her nervous and he needed her to act in a normal manner.

After a quick meal of burgers and fries for Carter and Miss Volasko, while Mick had grilled cheese with tomatoes, it was time to get on the road. Mick dropped his Caddy off at his home and put it in the garage, and then the happy threesome headed for Palmdale in Carter's car. The city in the desert was located about sixty miles to the north-east of Los Angeles.

The traffic on the I-14 Freeway, which is always congested, was worse than normal and it took Carter two hours for the normal one hour trip. Following directions provided by Miss Volasko, Carter pulled up in front of a house that was partially burned down and the half that wasn't burnt was covered in yellow crime scene tape.

Carter asked Miss Volasko if she was sure of the address. Her response was, "Carter, this house belongs to Helen and Bob Doyle. They're old friends of the family. Am I sure of the address? You're damn right I'm sure of the address."

"Okay, then we need to find the local police station and find out just what happened here."

Mick said, "I got a bad feeling boss."

Before Carter had a chance to put his car back in drive and step on the gas, Miss Volasko opened her door quickly and got out.

Carter yelled out, "What the hell are you doing?"

Starting to walk towards the front porch of the house she said, "I want to see what that notice next to the front door says."

As Carter opened his door and stepped out, he heard the whoop, whoop, whoop, of the Police Car that had just pulled up behind his and he said, "Ah shit!"

Mick laughed, "Hey, now you don't have to find them, they found you."

Carter said softly, "Funny, very funny."

Over the loud speaker of the Police Car the officer said, "Ma'am, return to your vehicle please, that is a posted police crime scene. If you attempt to cross that tape you will be arrested."

Miss Volasko stopped walking and turned around and saw Carter waving her back to the car.

The driver of the Police Car got out and walked towards Carter. Stopping about five feet in front of him, the officer asked, "Sir, what is your interest in that building?"

"Officer, my passenger is an old friend of the family and she was going to pay them a visit. We are shocked to see that the house had been engulfed in a fire. I hope everyone got out before there were any casualties."

"Actually sir, there were several casualties. If possible, your passenger might be some help in identifying two of the victims."

Hearing what the officer had said, Miss Volasko held her hand up to her mouth and said, "Oh my God!"

The officer asked, "Sir, if you would please follow me to the Police Station, it would be appreciated."

As they followed the Police Car, Carter told Miss Volasko, "Don't volunteer any information. Your sister may not be one of the victims. But if she is, please don't acknowledge it at this time."

With tears coming down her cheeks, "Are you crazy, you expect me to just ignore the fact that my sister could be lying in the morgue? Fuck you Carter! Do you hear me? Fuck you!"

The trip to the Police Station took only a few minutes, and when they all were escorted in, they were met by two detectives who introduced themselves. Det. Stan Toler and Det. Richard Fields led them to an interrogation room and then left them alone for about ten minutes before returning.

Carter stood and introduced himself handing Det. Toler one of his cards. Miss Volasko and Mick introduced themselves as well and they all sat at the table. Holding a notebook Det. Toler said, "Miss Volasko, I understand you were friends with the Doyles?"

"Yes Detective, I have known Helen and Bob Doyle since I was a teenager."

"I'm sorry to tell you ma'am, but both Helen and Robert Doyle were positively identified as two of the victims that perished in the fire three nights ago. There are still two unidentified victims that you might be able to help us with."

"Detective, I'm not familiar with any of the Doyles close friends, but I'm willing to see if I know the other two victims."

The walk to the city morgue was a short one. It only took a few minutes to cross the street to the Phillips Mortuary, the temporary city morgue. The mortuary was being used until the construction was completed on the new city complex being built a mile down the road.

Before viewing the bodies, Det. Toler explained, "Miss Volasko, the first unidentified male victim had his throat cut and he bled out on the living room floor."

Carter cut in and said, "Hold it Detective, what the hell does that have to do with a house fire?"

"Before we go any further, maybe I should explain a little of what we found at the scene after the fire department put out the fire and called us."

"I think that would be a good place to start."

"Okay, you noticed that the front of the house was still intact. The major part of the fire was to the rear two thirds of the structure. Entering the front door the first victim we found was Mr. Doyle, who had been shot several times in the chest and most likely died instantly. In his right hand we found a drywall razor knife covered with blood. Ten feet away we found victim number two, a male with several stab wounds and his throat cut from ear to ear. Neither man had been burned from the fire. In the kitchen, victim number three was found partially burned over 50% of her body, but she was identified as Helen Doyle and it appeared she died of a stroke. Victim number four was the worst of the fire victims but she was dead before the fire ever started. The woman had been severely tortured with several of her fingers cut off and even the nipples on her breasts had been snipped off. She had been tied to a chair and left to burn in the fire. First we will show you the male and see if you recognize him."

The blood had been washed from the body and the skin looked white and very chalky, but it was no one that Miss Volasko knew. Victim number four was rolled up to the viewing window and the sheet was pulled back slowly exposing the severely burned face and head of a woman.

Miss Volasko turned away quickly and leaned into the open arms of Carter and said, "Please take me away from here."

After the body was covered again, the detective asked, "I'm sorry you had to see that ma'am, but do you know who she is? Can you identify her?"

Taking a few deep breaths, Miss Volasko said, "No detective, I don't know who she is, I'm sorry but it's so gruesome. Can we get out of here now please?"

Walking back to the room they had been in earlier, Det. Toler handed Miss Volasko one of his cards and said, "This investigation will remain open. If you happen to think of something that might help, please call. I'm sorry for the loss of your friends. Hopefully we will be able to find the person or persons responsible."

Mick walked along with the group not saying anything until they returned to the car. Breaking the silence in the car, Mick said, "That woman didn't tell her killers anything. They tortured her to death and she couldn't tell them what they wanted. My guess is that she didn't know."

Carter said, "I'm sorry Regina, but I don't remember her from the wedding. Was that your sister?"

With tears now streaming down her face, Regina said "Yes Mr. Carter. That was Connie in there."

"I'm so sorry you had to find out that way."

Mick asked, "Where to now boss?"

Carter asked, "Are you alright Regina, do you want to stop somewhere for a drink or something else?"

Regina said, "I'm not alright, but I will be. We need to get back to the freeway and head for Lancaster, Mr. Carter."

"Please call me Don, Regina."

"On second thought Don, I could use a drink, and you can call me Reggie."

18

The city of Lancaster, CA, located just a few miles north of Palmdale, has many housing developments that started springing up in the late seventies. Most of the land in that area is still known for being ranchland with beautiful tall mountains as a backdrop. Connie and Dan McKay had lived on a fifteen acre ranch on a dead-end road at the foot of one of those beautiful mountains.

The ranch house on the property was very small considering how large the property was, but it was cozy and fit the needs of the childless couple. A hay barn, tool shed and coral were also on the property, built most likely by the previous owner.

Reggie Volasko had only visited her sister at the ranch a couple of times over the years, so it took her a few mistakes in her directions to Carter to find the correct road leading into their place.

Driving up to the front of the house, everything at first looked very normal and serene. Carter pointed out that the front door was partially opened and the window next to the door had been broken into. The porch, running along the front of the house was littered with broken patio furniture and tumbleweed that had blown there by the high winds that were common for the area.

Getting out of the car, Mick said, "I hope you have a weapon with you, I don't like the feel of this place Donny Boy. Keep your eyes open for trouble."

Reggie said, "Oh you're crazy" as she got out of the car and walked to the front door, pushing it open.

Standing in the doorway, Reggie said, "Oh my God, this place looks like a bomb went off in here."

While Mick walked around to the back of the house, Carter and Reggie entered and walked around slowly studying the mess before them.

It was obvious that someone had searched the home and it didn't appear that they located what they were searching for because they tore everything apart. Chair and couch cushions had been torn open, and the living room carpet had been stripped off the floor and piled in a corner of the room. The plaster drywalls had been cut open and the desk in the far left corner had the empty drawers stacked on top of it. The TV console had the back ripped open and sat with the front facing the wall.

Walking into the bedroom they found a similar mess with clothes thrown on the floor and shelves in the closets raked clean. The mattress and box spring had been cut open and all the dresser drawers dumped on the floor. The plaster walls had been cut and smashed open with large holes exposing the wall studs.

The same kind of mess was found in the kitchen with anything and everything just dumped on the floor, and drawers pushed to the side of the room. Bags of flour and sugar were dumped on the floor and some of their contents flung around making it obvious that the person or persons responsible were very angry.

Mick had come in the back door to the kitchen and said, "The barn out back has also been torn apart. You have to wonder if they found what they were after or just left disgusted?"

Carter said, "From the looks of everything, I don't think they found the eggs. You know, that's what they were searching for."

Mick smiled and said, "If you remember, Donny Boy, the way that Irishman's brain worked. I bet he hid those damn eggs in a place no one would find without a map."

Carter thought about it a few minutes as he walked around the house and then said, "Hey Mick, do you remember that scavenger hunt Dan put together that Halloween in Fort Hood? He was good at that shit, wasn't he?"

Reggie asked, "So you're saying Connie's husband may have left a map around here somewhere?"

Carter picked up an overturned kitchen chair and sat looking around the room. "Maybe not a map, but I'll bet he left some kind of clue."

Mick laughed and said, "I wouldn't put it past him, Donny Boy, to do just that."

Reggie said, "It's simple then, all we need to do is find the first clue."

Carter said, "You didn't know your brother in law that well, did you Reggie? He was a conniving bastard who loved to play mind games?"

"Where do you want to start, Donny Boy?"

"Tell you what Mick, let's start with the living room and slowly sift through every piece of crap out there."

Many hours of searching had turned up nothing that looked like a clue. Even the barn revealed nothing but garden tools and a few bales of hay.

The hay had undoubtedly been there a very long time because Reggie was sure they didn't have any horses or cows. The door on the shed next to the barn was partially open and the interior small and completely empty.

Connie and Dan McKay were hoarders in a small way, mainly because of the size of their home. Using the barn to store boxes or anything valuable was out of the question because of field mice and rats. Any paper products such as documents or pictures would be chewed up or destroyed by the rodents, so those things were kept in the house closets.

For some reason, Connie and Dan had saved old letters and photos from friends and bound them with elastic bands. They also saved advertisements from the local stores in town, greeting cards, paid bills, and piles of old newspaper articles. Carter had looked through all of the material, one piece at a time and discovered nothing.

Working with only the light provided by a couple kerosene lamps, it was a little after midnight when Carter said, "Okay guys, let's call it a night. We can continue the search tomorrow. I spotted a Holiday Inn just off the freeway in Palmdale so we can check in there for the night. Let's all sleep on this and try to figure out where he may have hid the clue. There's got to be something we missed."

19

Carter and Mick were sharing a room with double beds, while Reggie slept in the room next door. The night went by quickly and when Carter rolled out of bed in the morning, he looked for Mick but he was gone. Looking around the room, Carter saw a note sticking out of his shoe that Mick had put on the table. The note read, "Donny Boy, I went to pick up some breakfast. Be back soon."

It was a half hour later when Mick returned with three coffees, a dozen donuts and a quart of orange juice. Reggie was sitting at the table talking with Carter when Mick returned with the makeshift breakfast. Carter looked in the bag Mick was carrying, "What, no bacon and eggs?"

Mick smiled, "easier to eat these.

Carter and Reggie shared the coffee with their donuts, while Mick drank the orange juice and between the three of them they finished off eight donuts.

Reggie asked, "Hey Mick, don't think I didn't appreciate the donuts, but didn't they have any bagels?

Mick laughed and said, "Bagels! I ain't Jewish lady. I was brought up a Roman Catholic and we ate donuts for breakfast. Hell I didn't even know what a bagel was until I joined the army. To me, that's Jewish food. I got nothing against it. I just never developed a taste for those things."

Carter looked at his friend and said, "What are you? nuts? Bagels and cream cheese is a great way to start a morning. Christians eat bagels too. Every year at Christmas, I....... That's it Mick, I think you just hit on something! I don't remember. How religious was Dan?"

"You mean like believing in God or going to church?" Mick asked.

"No, no. Like, how did he get along with other nationalities? From what I remember, he used to look down on anyone who didn't act or believe as he did. And man, if you weren't the same color as his bright white ass, he just tolerated you. Is that what you remember too?"

Mick laughed and said, "Hey, I was brought up a Catholic, but I get along with all people. That

Irish prick was a damn bigot. If a person was black, brown, yellow or red he didn't want anything to do with them."

Carter asked, "What about Jews? How did he feel about Jewish people Mick? I think I remember him always putting down Jewish people, didn't he?"

"Yeah, you're right Donny Boy. Remember Horowitz? He never did anything to the Irishman, but every time we had a party at the house at Fort Hood, Dan excluded him because he was a Jew."

"Reggie, what about your sister, was she bigoted towards other people different from her?"

"Well, I think she was, but she never let on to others."

Carter said, "We need to get back to that house right away. I think I know where the clue is, let's go! You two grab all our shit and I'll go pay the bill. I'll meet you both at the car."

They were only about five minutes away from the motel when Carter's car phone started ringing. Carter said, "You answer it Mick."

Mick picked up the phone from the center console and said, "Mickey's Pizza, what's your order?"

Annie Dugan laughed and said, Very funny Mick-Man. Put Mr. C. on the phone. I need to talk with him now."

"She says she has to talk to you boss. No pizza today."

Taking the phone, Carter said, "Good morning sweetheart. What's so important?"

"Mr. Carter. That Det. Croft was here at the office yesterday looking for you. He told me you better come in to see him this morning or he's going to issue a warrant for your arrest. He scares me, Mr. Carter."

"I'll call him when I get off the phone with you Annie. Don't worry about him anymore. What else ya got?"

"That Mr. Creshanko called and left a number for you to call him back as soon as possible. I told him you had to go out of town on an emergency, but if you called I would let you know."

Carter repeated Creshanko's phone number as Annie gave it to him and Mick wrote it down. "Was there anything else sweetheart?"

"Oh yeah, some guy named Boris called a couple of times yesterday and said it was important for you to call him, but he didn't leave a number. When I asked him for it, he said you had it."

"Don't worry Annie, everything's going fine and you're doing a great job. We should be back tonight. Don't give out my number, but call me if you need me, okay?"

"Okay Mr. Carter, I'll take care of things here. Please don't forget to call that detective. You have his number right?"

Carter laughed and said, "Don't worry, I got it. Oh, how does this phone sound?"

"Well it seems to fade a little, but it's not bad for a car phone."

"Okay Annie, only call me if it's very important. Bye sweetheart."

Annie said, "Wait, wait, there's one more thing Mr. Carter. A letter came for you yesterday marked urgent, so I opened it."

"Who is it from Annie?"

"The envelope says, H & B Doyle, and it's a Palmdale address, but inside, the letter is from someone named Connie McKay."

"Listen carefully Annie. I want you to go next door to the exterminator's office and use their phone. Make some excuse like our phone isn't working, then call me back. Please, no questions. Just do it. Then I want you to read the letter to me."

Sounding confused, "Why Mr. C.?"

"Annie, please, just do it."

Two minutes later, Carter's phone rang.

Pulling over to the side of the road, Carter put the car in park, answered the phone, and shut off the engine.

Mick asked, "What's up boss?"

"A letter from Dan's wife Connie was sent to the office."

Reggie leaned forward from the back seat and said, "You got a letter from my sister?"

Carter fiddled with his car phone, turning up the volume, holding it so everyone could hear, then said, "Okay Annie, read the letter into the phone, but speak loud please."

"*Dear Mr. Carter. Danny told me to contact you if anything happened to him. Well he was killed by people who were trying to find something valuable that Dan had. I'm sure he didn't tell them where it was hidden. I know because they're looking for me to tell them, but I don't know what or where the thing is hidden. Danny said he left a trail for you to follow. Those people wrecked my house in Lancaster so I'll be moving to New York where my sister lives. I don't know what it means, but he said, Separate the Jews from the Christians and you may get some direction. Danny always liked to play games and talk in riddles, but Christians and Jews, I have no idea what he's talking about. Danny trusted you Mr. Carter, and so do I. I'll call you once I get settled in New York. Good luck, Connie McKay.*"

Annie asked, "Did you get that okay Mr. Carter?"

"Yes Annie, thank you. I'll call you later today, bye sweetheart."

Sitting quietly for a couple of minutes, and seeing the tears well up in Reggie's eyes, Carter said, "I'm sorry Reggie."

"Thank you Carter, they can't hurt her anymore."

Taking out his notebook from his pocket he looked up Det. Croft's private number and called. Holding up a finger to his lips he motioned to Mick and Reggie, "Shush."

Answering on the second ring, Carter heard, "Croft here."

"Croft, its Carter. What the hell do you want now?"

"Carter, where the hell are you?"

"I'm out of town and it's none of your business where I am. Now, what the hell do you want?

"What I want Carter, is you in my office today, you got that, wise guy?"

"Don't try to push your weight on me Croft, I'll be back in town tomorrow and I'll come by to see you. Are we done, I have an appointment to keep."

"You better be here tomorrow Carter or…."

Carter disconnected and said to Mick, What an asshole."

Restarting the car Carter put it in drive and floored it, burning rubber back on to the freeway surface. Once up to the speed limit Carter asked, "Reggie, are you sure your sister was a bigot?"

"As much as I hate to admit it, yes she was. I don't know where she got it from because both our parents were free thinkers who believed in freedom for everyone. Please Carter. Don't think because my sister was like that, that it ran in the family."

"Okay Reggie you got a deal. Please, enough with calling me Carter, call me Don, I prefer it."

Mick spoke up trying to ease the tension, "Hey Donny Boy, what should I call you?"

"Your lordship would be nice Mick."

"That ain't going to happen, boss man."

They all laughed and then Mick asked, "So what's up with all this bigot crap? Where the hell are you going with it?"

"Wait until we get to the house Mick. If I'm right about this, we're going to be involved in a treasure hunt put together by the Irishman, and I think I know where it starts. Reggie's sister confirmed something I was thinking about."

For the next ten minutes no one spoke until they pulled up in front of the Lancaster house. As they were all getting out of the car Mick said, "It's show time."

Carter was the first one into the house and he walked straight to a big box that had been in the closet. It had been dumped out at the first search but Carter had put it all back in the box as he checked it for clues when they first arrived. Once again Carter dumped the contents on the floor and picked up a bundle of greeting cards.

Mick and Reggie were watching closely when Carter said, "I noticed something strange about this pile of cards last night, but it didn't sink in until Reggie asked about bagels. Then you, Mick, told me you weren't Jewish. Knowing what a damn bigot the Irishman was, I couldn't understand why he saved this."

Holding up a Chanukah card that was mixed in with all the Christmas cards, Carter said, "Why would a couple of stone bigots save a Jewish holiday card?"

When Carter opened the card there was something written in a language that he couldn't read and said, "There's something written here but I can't make it out."

Mick looked at it and said, "I think it's Latin. Can you read Latin Reggie?"

Reggie looked and said, "Its Latin okay."

Carter asked, "So what's it say?"

Reggie brought the card over to the window for more light and read, "Twice a day it points the way, with the one that works just fine. To find which way and time of day, find the one that no longer tells time."

Mick asked, "What the hell does that mean?"

Carter hesitated a few seconds and said, "Clocks, one working, one not. Let's find them."

Walking through the house and checking each room carefully, the only working clock they found was one that was lying on the floor in the corner of the living room. The face of the clock was broken and the battery had been knocked out of it. Mick put the battery back in and it started working again.

Mick said, "Ya know, out in the barn, there's an old grandfather clock that's leaning against the back wall. It looks like it's been there a long time because there's all kinds of shit piled around it."

Reggie said, "I saw an old clock radio in the bedroom closet up on the shelf with its cord wrapped around it and the plug cut off. Do you think maybe......?"

Carter said, "Let's check 'em' out. What do we have to lose?"

The clock radio from the closet was an old beat up radio with the plastic cover on the clock part removed. The short hour hand was pointing to nine and the large hand on twelve. Walking out to the barn to check the grandfather clock, it was easy to see that it must have been sitting out there for a long time by the thick coating of dust covering it. Carter wiped away the thick dust and saw the little hand pointing to the nine and the big hand on twelve.

Carter said, "Okay, now we just have to figure out which wall the clock in the living room was on. Look at it this way. If we find which wall the clock that was working was on, and then see where the little hand is pointing at nine, we have a direction."

Mick laughed and said, "Hey Donny Boy, look at it this way; its got to be one of only four directions we have to search."

Carter folded his arms across his chest and said, "Brilliant, Einstein. You must have been the smart one in your graduating class at school."

20

Standing just inside the front doorway of the house, all three of them studied the walls to try to imagine where the clock would have been displayed. By smashing and cutting the drywall plaster, the searchers before them had destroyed any markings of where the clock had been mounted. Picturing the clock on each wall, they then searched to the left of that position.

The search was hopeless; not knowing whether they were supposed to look inside or outside of the house just made it more confusing.

Carter asked, "Reggie, try to remember from your previous visits where the clock had been mounted."

"I have Don, but it was so long ago I can't recall."

As Mick searched through piles of papers and photographs that had been on the floor of the living room closet, he yelled out, "Bingo! I got it."

Carter said, "You got what?"

"How about a picture of what's her name, Reggie's sister and the Irishman standing in the living room with the clock mounted on the wall behind them?"

Reggie, with an angry tone said, "Her name was Connie, you dork, not what's her name."

"I'm sorry Reggie, I just forgot."

Carter asked, "Where were they standing Mick?"

"Right next to the front door and the clock can be seen just over Connie's right shoulder."

Pointing at the wall next to the front door, Carter said, "Okay that would put the clock right about here."

Drawing an imaginary line to the left of where the clock would have been mounted, they now knew the exact direction to search. Since the only thing to the left was the corner of the room where the wall had already been ripped open, their search would have to continue outside.

Carter, still following that imaginary line, walked to a tool shed attached to the side of the barn and now noticed the torn-off hasp and padlock lying on the ground that he paid no attention to on their first visit the day before.

When he pulled open the partially opened two doors, he was surprised to see nothing but empty space. Reggie and Mick were standing behind Carter and said together, "What the hell?"

Carter said, "Okay, maybe it's pointing at the barn."

As they started walking towards the barn doors, Mick said, "Wait a minute, there is nothing in that shed and yet they had to pry the lock and hasp off. Why would a completely empty shed be locked up tighter than a drum?"

"Okay Mick," Carter said, "You check it out while Reggie and I check out the barn."

After a couple hours, Reggie, Carter and Mick had moved just about everything from the left side of the barn and came up with nothing.

Returning to the tool shed, Mick was only gone about ten minutes when he came back to the barn and stood quietly in the doorway. Clearing his throat loudly a couple times until Carter and Reggie looked at him, he said with a little smugness in his voice, "You guys can stop looking now. It's not in here."

Carter asked, "How do you know it's not in here?"

Mick said, "Because I found it in the shed."

Reggie asked, "The eggs?"

Laughing loudly Mick said, "No, but I'm pretty sure it's another damn clue. That Irishman had one hell of an imagination."

"Show me what you found Mick," Carter said.

Walking out of the barn and standing in front of the empty shed, Carter said, "Well, what have you got, it's empty?"

"Step in boss and I'll show you."

Standing in the middle of the shed Carter said, "So?"

Mick laughed and said, "Stretch out your arms, touch the rear wall with your finger tip and reach towards the opening and guess what the distance is from front to back."

"Okay funny man, it's about six feet, now what?"

"Let's go outside and do the same thing out there, and tell me what's wrong with your measurement."

Stepping to the outside of the shed, Carter leaned against it and stretched out with arms extended all the way and said, "It's about a foot longer. Son of a bitch, there's a phony wall in there."

"Right boss, let's go back in. I'll show you what else I found."

Stepping back into the shed, Mick said, "Look at each corner of the back wall and tell me what you see."

Carter looked at each corner, smiled and said, "Drywall screws."

"Yep, everything else is nailed together, but the rear wall has four drywall screws, one in each corner. I'll bet you that if we remove those screws we're going to find something hidden in there. What do you think?"

Carter started walking out of the shed and said, "I think we need a Phillips head screwdriver."

Mick said, "I saw one in the box next to the desk in the house."

It only took Carter a few minutes to find the screwdriver and get back to the shed and remove the screws from the wall. Prying on one end of the wall, he slowly worked it back and forth until he was able to remove it completely. Sitting on a couple of bricks was a black leather bag similar to a doctor's bag. It appeared to have been there a long time judging by the heavy coat of dust and spider webs.

Opening the bag, Carter removed an envelope and tore it open. In bold letters it read, *"To whom it may concern. My guess would be that it's you Carter. Don't ask why, but I'm sure that psycho Mick is right by your side. Connie, I'm sure that you are there also. Here's the story. In the bag is ten thousand in cash, along with enough jewelry to sell for many years to come.*

"I know you're asking, 'what the hell did he do with the eggs?' I'll get to that in a little while. First, the eggs were never meant to be sold. My intent was always to return them to the Russian Museum in Moscow. I know that's hard to believe Carter, but that's what I now want you to do. There will be a reward that you can divide up anyway you wish. Many people have given their lives because of those eggs and now it will be an additional part of their history.

"Next on the agenda is a personal favor. A man named Serge Creshanko is responsible for the death of my two friends in the military who were brutally beaten when those eggs were stolen. My guess would be that he has ordered the death of many more to this point in time. I'm sure you and the psycho can figure out a way, 'legally,' to terminate his existence.

"Now Carter, since you figured out my little time game to get this far, here's another one for you. Adding the time on the clock that got you here, the temperature water boils at, your age when we first met, and how many miles round trip we had to travel to get the corn whisky at old man Weber's farm from the house off post. Now, add that up and then subtract the year of my first car. You remember. It was the same as your old Dodge. Put all this together using your head for math and it will give you direction. Think back to where we *were standing when that tornado came through Gatesville, Texas. Use a compass and your figures in degrees; it will take you to your next clue in about one hundred and fifty paces. One more thing Carter. Make sure Connie gets her share."*

Mick laughed, "And he calls me a psycho."

Carter asked, "Hey Mick, you don't have a compass with you by any chance do you?"

"Sure boss, I got one right here in my pocket."

"Good Mick, I was wondering where the hell we could get one."

"That was sarcasm Donny Boy, couldn't you recognize it?"

"Okay smartass, so where do we get a compass?"

Reggie spoke up and said, "I saw a sporting goods store when we turned off the freeway earlier. They should have one there."

Carter said, "Mick take a ride with Reggie and go pick up a compass while I hunt around here. Please, no Cracker Jack compass; get something that's fairly accurate. Why don't you pick us up a few burgers or something to eat, I'm getting a little hungry."

"Okay we'll go boss, but when we get back you have to explain how the hell that Irishman knew we would be the ones to find the satchel and the shit inside."

"That I can't tell you Mick, because I have no idea. From the looks of that bag it had been in that hiding place a long time, so that means he put this together way before his death."

As Reggie looked and listened, she said nothing, but once again a slight smile appeared on her face. Then said, "Sometimes fate plays a hand in what we do."

Mick said, "Fate or no fate, he had to have a friggin crystal ball to know that we would be the ones to figure out his little hiding place."

This time Carter smiled, "Maybe we'll find out when we find the eggs."

21

Placing the bag containing the jewelry in the trunk of the car, Carter then walked into the house and started going through some of the papers that had been in the desk as Mick and Reggie drove away.

Only twenty minutes had gone by when he heard a car drive up in front of the house. Thinking it was a little too fast for Mick and Reggie to be returning, Carter slowly walked to the front door and was greeted by a big guy pointing a gun at his face.

The man asked, "Are you Carter?"

"That depends. Who are you?"

"I'm the guy who's going to put a bullet in your head if you try anything funny, asshole."

"Well in that case, yeah I'm Carter. What can I do for you big guy?"

"Mr. Creshanko would like to talk with you. Move it funny man, to the car."

Another man Carter assumed was the driver was standing near the open driver's side of the black Lincoln town car. The rear door was opened wide and as Carter approached, he heard, "Step inside Mr. Carter and be seated."

Carter got in and sat next to Serge Creshanko and said, "Are you and your crew just out slumming or was this a planned trip?"

"This is not the time for humor Mr. Carter. Have you located the jeweled eggs yet?"

"Well Serge, it appears that I'm re-searching places that you have already searched. You know my time is valuable, yet you never informed me about this place. You could have saved me some time and told me about this location in one of our earlier conversations."

"Enough of your stalling bullshit Mr. Carter, what have you found?"

"What I found sir is the mess your people left before I arrived here. Any clues that I might have found have been destroyed by your bungling idiots. Now, is there is anything else you haven't told me? If there is, I'd like to know now."

"And where are Miss Volasko and your assistant?" Creshanko asked.

"Oh, they went to get lunch. With all the overtime I've been putting in I keep forgetting to eat. You know, one must keep up one's strength."

"Mr. Carter, this is not the time for jokes. I am not in a humorous frame of mind. Please cooperate or I will have Ivan and Randolph help you with your memory."

"If you can hold off your goons for awhile and use a little patience, there may be a 'burger' in the bag for you when they return."

Creshanko was truly not in a humorous mood and he called to both his men, "Ivan, Randolph, would you both see if you can put Mr. Carter in a more serious mood."

Carter saw what was coming next and said, "Wait a minute, wait a minute. You're losing sight of what your true desires are here. The eggs! That's what's important here. You want them and I'm getting closer to finding them, so tell your two mountain men to back off!"

Holding up his hand so his men could see, Creshanko said, "Speak Mr. Carter and dispense with the jokes."

"Please, come with me into the house," Carter asked.

Creshanko said, "As you wish, but I warn you, don't be foolish and continue on your path of leading me on Mr. Carter."

Carter was trying to stall for time hoping that Mick and Reggie would see what was going on as they returned and possibly turn the situation around. Pointing through the doorway at the mess in the house, Carter said, "I assume that was some of your handy work?"

"Yes, we thoroughly searched the house, as you can tell."

"Next time Creshanko, you should leave the searching to people who know what they are doing instead of trained gorillas." Turning and looking at the big man next to his boss, Carter said, "No offense guy, but it's just not your thing."

"You're wasting my time Mr. Carter. Show me what you have found."

"What I have discovered, Creshanko, is that the eggs are not here but I am piecing together clues that Mr. McKay has left for me to follow. Once I have deciphered what he meant I will continue with my search. Now what I insist from you is for you to get the hell out of here and give me twenty-four hours and I will have them in my possession."

"You, I believe, are wasting my time Mr. Carter. You are stalling, thinking I am a fool."

"Creshanko, you have searched for so long for those eggs. Will twenty-four more hours be so great a time that you would risk losing them forever?"

While the limo driver had stayed with the car, Carter, Creshanko and Ivan were the ones who entered the house. Carter had no idea what his next move would be, so when he heard the gun shots from outside, he said, "I believe the cavalry has arrived, Creshanko."

Looking out the front window, Creshanko saw his driver lying in front of the car spread eagle face down with Reggie sitting on his back and a gun pointed at the back of his head.

Rushing out of the front door with his gun in his hand, Ivan was met by Mick who quickly dropped the big man with a swift swing of a two-by-four to the man's knees followed by a kick to his head.

Picking up the big man's gun, Mick looked at Carter and said, "I didn't know you were going to invite guests for lunch boss."

Carter asked, "I'm so glad to see you, but when the hell did you get back?"

"Reggie and I spotted them when they turned off the freeway, but it took us a little time to figure out a game plan."

Carter asked, "What about Randolph out there?"

"Who?" Mick asked.

"The driver," Carter said.

"Oh he's fine, maybe he'll have a headache but it's better than dead."

Creshanko finally spoke and asked, "And what may I ask is your plan for me Mr. Carter?"

Carter said, "You just don't get it Creshanko, I got a job to do, a job for you, you're still my client. Now you and your two monkeys can get in your car and get the hell out of here. When I find your eggs, I'll call you. By the way, the finder's fee just went up another five thousand. If you continue to harass me and play your stupid games, I'll leave you to find those eggs yourself."

Confused about what had just taken place, Creshanko and his men got back into the town car. Putting down the window he said to Carter, "You are a strange sort of man Mr. Carter. I will be waiting for your call."

Carter said with a smile, "Start counting out your finder's fee comrade."

"We have a financial agreement, Mr. Carter and I will hold you to that agreement."

"Hey Creshanko, the fee just went up *another* five thousand. If you don't get the hell out of here now, it will be an additional ten thousand."

Watching the Lincoln town car drive away, leaving behind it clouds of dust, Carter turned to Mick and Reggie and asked, "Does this mean you didn't find a compass?"

Reggie said, "What?"

Carter added, "No lunch either?"

Carter and Mick looked at each other and then started to laugh.

Reggie said, "You guys are sick."

Carter said, "No Reggie, just trying to make light of the moment. I'll tell you what, this time we all take a ride and pick up the compass. We can stop at a restaurant for something to eat. Then I'll tell you two what I found in those papers by the desk."

22

Sitting in a Denny's restaurant and looking at a ledger that belonged to Dan McKay, Reggie asked Carter, "Don, how did they miss this when they were searching the house?"

"The thin ledger was disguised as a children's book and had a fake Donald Duck cover. It was grouped together with other kids' books. For some reason the idiots searching the house didn't realize that the McKay's didn't have any children."

Mick asked, "So. What do you make of it Donny Boy?'

Carter sat back in his chair, sipped his coffee and said, "I don't know Mick. It may be just another one of the Irishman's little curveballs to get whoever found it heading in another direction.

Either way, we have to consider the possibility that we're on a wild goose chase and he's making fools out of all of us."

Reggie asked, "So you think it's possible that he planted that to mislead anyone, other than us, who found it, in a wrong direction?"

"That could be Reggie, but I guess the only way we'll find out is to play out the other crap."

Mick said, "Well let's get the hell out of here, buy a compass, and get back to the hunt."

Forty-five minutes later as they all stood on the porch back at the ranch, Carter looked at the compass he held in his hand and said, "This door is facing west; adding my age when I met Dan which was 22; water boils at 212; the clock time 9, I come up with 243 degrees on the compass. Figure in 26 miles round trip to old man Weber's farm and I get 269. The car Dan is talking about was a 1948 Dodge. So if I subtract 48, I come up with 221 degrees.

Mick, who was standing on Carter's right, said, "To me it looks like that tall tree in the center of that line of trees along the dirt road, that's approximately the direction we need to go."

Walking about one hundred and fifty yards to a row of eucalyptus trees, Carter, Mick, and Reggie looked around the base of the tallest tree but noticed nothing unusual about it. Looking up into the large dried out bare tree, Reggie asked, "Is that a bird house up near the center about halfway up?"

Climbing up the tree, Mick reached the branch where the bird house was mounted. It was camouflaged by many dried out smaller branches to make it look like a squirrels nest. Calling down to Carter he said, "It would be awfully hard for a bird to get into this thing, there ain't no hole in it."

After breaking the bird house loose from the branch, Mick tossed it down to Carter, and then climbed back down.

The bird house was screwed together and meant to fool anyone looking up at it from the ground. Returning to the house Carter said, "Another one of his damn clues in this stupid game."

When he removed the screws from the roof of the bird house, Carter found an envelope which contained a note. *Well you made it this far and you're getting closer. Carter, remember when we busted Capt. Stanton? His hiding place for the drugs was a real cool one wasn't it? We fried that chicken bastard, didn't we? Good hunting."*

Carter laughed and said, "That son of a bitch is going to run us around this property playing his dumb ass games. We need to go back to the house."

Walking in the front door, Carter headed straight for the kitchen. Opening the refrigerator freezer he was surprised to see it completely empty. Looking at Mick, he said, "When Dan and I busted a captain who was a suspect for dealing drugs at Fort Hood, the guy was hiding his shit in the freezer. I thought for sure something would be here."

Mick said, "The barn. I saw an old refrigerator out there lying on its side."

A couple minutes passed, and the three of them were moving trash that had been piled up around an old beat up refrigerator that looked like it had been there a long time. Once Carter and Mick turned it on its back, Carter opened the freezer door and looked at several moldy nasty looking packages of frozen chicken.

Lifting them out one by one, opening them and dumping the contents on the ground, the third one was the charm. Again, an envelope sealed in a plastic sandwich bag. The note read, *"This key will open the box that gets you closer to the end of the game. Your next trip is to the Van Nuys Post Office where you will find the directions to another PO Box that contains what I wish returned to its rightful owners. The PO Box number in Van Nuys is the same as my wedding date to Connie. Thank you for your indulgence. I will always love you my sweet Connie. Dan.*

The drive back to the valley only took a little over an hour with the light traffic but finding a parking spot at the post office was very difficult. Once they parked the car, all three went into the post office and stood looking at the many rows of PO boxes.

Carter told Mick, "I think the Irishman got married on October ninth."

Reggie corrected him and said, "You're correct about it being October, but it was the seventh."

Mick said, "Okay, then that would be Box 107 correct?"

"Let's find 107," Carter said.

The search only took a couple of minutes and Reggie said, "Here it is, over here."

Trying the key in the lock they found it would not open. Then Carter said, "Wait a minute, how about one of the lower boxes, like the ones over in the corner. Try 1007."

In the next row of boxes on the lower level they found Box 1007. Carter inserted the key and turned it to the right, opening the box. The only thing in it was an envelope with a note and another key. The note was simple. "Our house number in Gatesville."

This time Mick took the key and walked to the next row of boxes and opened Box 2010. Removing a blue satchel with the letters TWA printed on it, Mick was surprised by its weight.

Opening the bag he saw only a white towel covering its contents. Lifting the towel a little at first, he then handed the bag to Carter who decided it was not the proper place to inspect the contents of the bag.

Reggie suggested going to Carter's home to inspect the contents but he said, "No, let's go to my office. We can secure the building and spot intruders much easier."

The drive from the post office only took twenty minutes with many turns to avoid the possibility of being followed. The truck repair shop had closed for the night and the gates were locked. Once inside the compound, Mick relocked the gate behind them and they all went up to the office.

Carter placed the satchel on his desk and started to remove the contents. The towel was only a cover. Next he removed four individually wrapped bundles covered in cotton and medical gauze. Under the bundles was another towel and when it was removed, it revealed wrapped piles of hundred dollar bills.

Unwrapping one of the cotton bundles, Carter and the others got their first look at what everyone was dying over. It was beautiful and there were three more in the bag which didn't add up with what Creshanko had told him. There were only supposed to be three eggs not four.

Now some of what he had read in the ledger made a little more sense. It was going to be a long night preparing what he needed to do to end this game. With the valuable prize he had in front of him, Carter knew he had to be extremely careful, because once it was discovered that he had the eggs, there was no reason for him or the others to remain alive.

Mick asked, "Now that we found them boss, what do we do with them?"

Reggie asked, "You're not going to turn them over to Creshanko are you?"

"No Reggie. For now they need to be put in a safe place until I can figure out what the hell to do with them."

Mick said, "Well let's see what they all look like, maybe we can hide them in plain sight."

Carter and Reggie looked at him and said, "What?"

23

Unwrapping all the eggs and setting them up on the desk in front of him, Carter said, "They sure are beautiful aren't they Mick?"

Mick smiled and said, "Yeah, if you like those kind of things. Me, I prefer my eggs over easy with hash browns and bacon."

Carter asked, "How about you Reggie?"

"What I see is lots of money that could last a lifetime for someone."

"Mick, I have an idea that may involve your uncle in New York and another Russian I'm pretty sure I can trust."

Mick laughed, "Remember what I told you boss, about dealing with my uncle. It could cost you your soul."

"Yeah I know. Why don't you take off Mick and get some rest, I'll give you a call in a few hours when I decide what to do next."

Carter told Reggie, "Keep an eye on the goods sweetheart. I'm going to walk down with Mick and lock the gate when he leaves."

Returning in about five minutes, Carter found Reggie sitting behind the desk and the eggs nowhere in sight. Still standing in the doorway Carter asked, "So it looks like you have your own plan, huh Reggie?"

"Carter, somehow I just don't think your plan will be very profitable for me, so yeah, I've decided to go it alone."

As Carter took one step slowly towards the desk Reggie lifted her hand from her lap and pointed a gun at him and said, "You can stop right there Carter. I do know how to use this, I don't want to kill you, but I will if you push me to it."

"Yeah I do know that you know how to use that Reggie. You see I saw your handy work at the Sportsmen's Lodge. So what happened, the fat guy fall out of your good graces?"

"Yeah well, the fat bastard decided he wanted more from me than I wanted to give. That dumb ass thought he could get drunk and rape me and get away with it."

"So you killed him for that?"

"Carter, when I left his room that night, he was still alive. He had one hell of a crack on his skull but he was still breathing. I whacked him in the head with his own gun and took it with me. The next morning when I checked on him he had been shot in the head and I took off."

"And what are your plans for me now Reggie?"

From the bathroom to Reggie's right, there came a crashing noise and when she turned and walked to open the door, Carter quickly ducked and ran out of the office door.

Running down the hallway after Carter, out onto the metal steps, Reggie never saw Mick when he came up behind her and grabbed her around the neck, disarming her.

Walking back up the steps Carter said, "You waited almost a little too long there Mick."

"Yeah well your neighbor in the pest control is going to be pissed at you. I threw a snow globe from his desk into the adjoining bathroom and splattered it on the wall."

Holding Reggie with one arm behind her back and the collar on her shirt, Mick walked her back into Carter's office and sat her down. Carter opened one of the desk drawers and removed two pairs of handcuffs and cuffed both of Reggie's wrists to the arms of the chair. Carter and Mick both sat down on the couch and Carter said, "I'm going to need a long vacation after this is over."

Reggie asked, "So Carter, what made you think *I* shot Gregor at the hotel and not one of Creshanko's people?"

"You never cleaned the weapon you were carrying. Remember at my house when I disarmed you. I looked at that little automatic before I handed it back to you. What I saw was blood on those nice white pearl handles. I never really trusted you, I was always prepared for you to turn on me, I just didn't know when. Once we found the eggs, I knew it could happen any time."

"So what are you going to do now?"

Laughing, Carter said, "For right now, I'm going to leave your ass in that chair."

"When you realize your mistake Carter, you're going to feel like a real ass."

Looking at Mick, Carter said, "Mick, I need you to take those eggs and stash them away somewhere safe. I have to get hold of Croft and have a long talk with him. I'll call you tomorrow and let you know what I decided to do."

"What about her, Donny Boy?"

"I'll have to figure that out also."

After rewrapping all the eggs that Reggie had just quickly stuffed in the satchel, Mick took off and left Carter just sitting staring at Reggie.

"What the hell am I going to do with you Reggie?"

"Carter, you're going to get yourself killed. You should have just let me take those damn eggs and go. I can't tell you anymore, but they would wind up where they are supposed to go."

"Right Reggie and you would make your little fortune as they were passed on."

"No, you don't understand Carter, but in time you will, and then you'll see how wrong you are."

24

Carter made the call to Det. Croft, and after a short conversation the detective sent a patrol car to pick up Reggie Volasko. Carter followed the patrol car to the Van Nuys police station and after four hours of interrogation, he was on his way back home for some long needed sleep.

Being awakened by his phone ringing at 9am was not something Carter was expecting, so he let the answering machine pick up as he listened. "Mr. Carter, it's Annie, I tried your car phone but you didn't answer. I don't know if you're home yet but we need to talk."

Before Annie went on, Carter picked up the phone and said, "Hi sweetheart, yeah I'm home, what's up?"

"Well first Mr. Carter, I hope you called that detective so you don't go to jail. Second, that nasty Russian man, Mr. Creshanko, called three times yesterday and threatened me. He told me he would come to the office and choke your number out of me. I'm scared of him Mr. Carter, you need to call him right away or I'm not going to the office today."

"Annie, I spent four hours last night with Det. Croft. As for Mr. Creshanko, I'm going to call him as soon as I get off the phone with you, I promise, and everything will be fine."

"Will you be going to the office this morning Mr. Carter?"

"Yes Annie, after my call to Creshanko, a nice hot shower and something to eat, and I'll be there. I should be in by eleven. Honest sweetheart, everything will be okay."

"Okay Mr. Carter. Is there anything you need me to do?"

"No Annie, just go in and answer the phone and handle things the way you have been. Bye Annie, see you soon."

"Bye Mr. Carter."

Carter did have a plan and it would take the help of Mick's uncle in New York. But first he needed to call Serge Creshanko and inform him that the time was getting very close for him to pick up his precious eggs.

On the third ring, Creshanko answered, "Yes, who's calling please?"

"Creshanko, it's Carter."

Mr. Carter, do you have my property yet, as promised?"

"They are very beautiful Creshanko, that's why I have them in a very safe place. They will remain there until we finish with our financial arrangement. With all that you have put me and my staff through, and considering their real worth, I will be expecting much more than we first agreed on."

"I don't like it that you are holding me up for an additional finder's fee, but that can be arranged Mr. Carter. Now when can I expect delivery?"

"Not so fast. The millions that you will receive for the diamond, ruby and emerald incrusted beauties will be far more than the two hundred thousand dollars you will be paying me for them."

"Are you out of your mind Mr. Carter? That sum is ridiculous I will not pay you anything near that."

"Look Creshanko don't try to bullshit me. I know what that Arab has offered to pay you for these damn eggs. My price is a small piddling of what you intend to get. Now unless you want me to sell these eggs on the open market, I suggest you do exactly what I tell you."

After a short silence, "As you wish Mr. Carter, what is it that you want from me?"

"The first thing you will do is stay by your phone. I will call you back within the hour with full instructions. Do you understand me clearly Creshanko? If you do anything other than what I tell you to do, you will never get your hands on those eggs. Is that clear enough for you?"

"You have made it very clear Mr. Carter."

"Fine Creshanko, now that we understand each other, I suggest you start working on the cash you will need. One more thing, do not call my office and threaten my assistant again, or you will find these precious eggs of yours scrambled, with a sledgehammer. I will not put up with your bullying tactics. Now is that also clear?

"Very clear Mr. Carter."

"Goodbye Creshanko."

After hanging up, Carter, still worried that his home phone might be tapped, went out to his car phone and called Annie. "Sweetheart, what I would like you to do is go to the office, turn on the answering machine, lock up the office and go home. Consider the next week off paid vacation time. I'll call in a couple of days and explain everything to you. I don't want you going back to the office for any reason. You got that."

"We can't afford to close the office for a week."

"We will Annie, we will. If you don't feel comfortable doing it, please just stay home."

"Thank you Mr. C. I would rather stay home because that man really scared me."

"It's okay Annie. I'll call you in a couple days. You did a great job these past few days keeping things together at the office. Bye Annie."

The next call Carter made from his car was to Mick, and he explained what he wanted his Uncle Vito to do. Mick said, "Now, let me make sure I got this clear. You want my uncle to collect two hundred thousand from Creshanko, in New York. Then you want him to call me back once he has the money in his possession. He gets to keep one hundred thousand as part of your gratitude and the other hundred thousand he delivers out here by one of his associates. Is that about it?"

"That's it in a nutshell Mick. Do you think he'll do it?"

"Sounds like a slam dunk to me Donny Boy. How could he refuse?"

"Mick do me a favor and call him right away and call me back."

"I'll call him as soon as I get off the phone with you."

"Now, another thing Mick, I studied that ledger last night before I got to bed. We need to meet some place so I can check out those eggs. It can't be my office or my house. You got any ideas? It needs to be a place that has a sink or a bathroom? Also I need you to bring along a small artist's brush and something else to wrap the eggs in."

Mick asked, "What about a motel for the place?"

"Okay, you got one in mind? We only need it for a couple hours?"

"Yeah, how about the Holiday Inn down the street from my house. I know the manager there, I'm sure he can fix us up?"

"Okay Mick, I know the place. How about we meet there at eleven? Meanwhile give your uncle a call."

"You got it boss, eleven it is. I'll call you right back after I talk to Uncle Vito."

Fifteen minutes later Carter answered the phone and heard Mick say, "Uncle Vito sends his regards and said he looks forward to meeting you when he flies out here for a visit after his business with Creshanko."

"Great Mick, I look forward to meeting him also. See you at eleven."

Carter's next call was to Serge Creshanko and he explained the details of how the money would be paid, and added, "I'm sure you know the price you would have to pay if you fuck with Vito Terratello."

"Mr. Carter, I'm very familiar with Vito Terratello and his very colorful reputation. I know, or should I say knew, people who crossed him. Everything will go just as you say. I assure you I am not a fool and I look forward to receiving my goods. You will be paid for your work just as you requested."

"Fine Creshanko, Vito will be calling me when he has the money in his possession. Enjoy your flight and I will be waiting for the conformation that the money has changed hands. Remember, you try anything stupid, and you will never see those precious eggs."

25

The room at the Holiday Inn was perfect for what Carter had to do. Besides the satchel containing the eggs, Mick brought along the few special items Carter had requested.

Not taking any chances about possibly being followed, both Mick and Carter drove around for well over an hour before going to the hotel. Mick had given Carter the room number and instructions where in the lot to park his car so he could watch from the balcony for anyone following him.

As the two men sat at a table in the suite that had been provided by the manager of the hotel, Carter looked around and said, "This is nice Mick. Please thank your friend for me."

Carter then removed the ledger he had found in the Lancaster house from his pocket and started to read it aloud from one particular page. "The power of the Nile will wash away a star from the heavens to reveal the true prize."

"What the hell does that mean Danny Boy?"

"I thought about this a lot Mick. After reading it over a few times, thinking about how that crazy Irishman's mind worked, there's only one explanation. The power of the Nile is water. One of the eggs has a star on it that will wash away with water. And if I'm wrong, I could fuck up the egg, simple as that."

"Suppose you *are* wrong Donny Boy? Do you really think water could screw it up?"

"Look Mick, I think that's why there's the fourth egg. Once the egg with the diamond has been discovered the clone can take its place."

"What clone?"

"Listen to this. "A clone will take its place but not for eternity."

"So you think the fourth egg doesn't really mean shit?"

Carter said, "Give that man a cigar."

Mick asked, "Any more words of wisdom from the book?"

"Yeah, something about the clone assuming the position until all has been returned to its rightful heir. Then the prize will shine once more."

"And what the hell does that mean?"

"You got me Mick."

"So what's next boss man?"

Carter laid out a towel on the table and removed all four eggs from the satchel. He said, "Okay Mick, would you get me a glass of water please and that little paint brush I asked you to pick up."

Mick asked, "You sure about this?"

"Hell no, but I'm going for it."

Holding the first jewel encrusted egg in his hand, Carter dipped the brush in the water and slowly brushed the seven stars, looking for some reaction, but nothing happened.

Each of the seven stars on all of the eggs had a small bright jewel in its center and Carter didn't know what to expect as the water was applied. He was hoping the water didn't cause the jewel to fall off and damage the egg.

With the second egg in hand, Carter applied the water as he did with the first, and again there was no reaction.

Mick asked, "So what the hell is it supposed to do?"

"I have no idea Mick."

Holding the third egg and brushing on the water, Carter noticed something different from the first two. Applying the water a second time, Carter noticed one of the stars disappear and then reappear. "Hey Mick watch this." Dipping the brush in the water and brushing it over the star, once again the star behind the jewel disappeared and then reappeared.

Mick said, "Holy crap."

Laying that egg off to the side, Carter picked up the fourth egg. He brushed water on all the stars and watched as there was no reaction to any of them. He knew then, he had found the egg with the diamond. Now he had to decide whether to continue with his plan he had formulated.

Mick smiled and asked, "What's next boss?"

Removing an ink marker from his pocket, Carter placed a small dot on the bottom of the diamond egg, and then packed them all back in the satchel, wrapping each one separately.

Leaving the Holiday Inn, they were very careful watching again to make sure they had not been followed.

Before getting into their cars, Carter said, "Mick, meet me at the Bank of America near my shop on Lankershim."

Carter's first step of the deception was to put the diamond egg, once he identified it, into his safe deposit box at his bank. The remaining three eggs would be turned over to Serge Creshanko once the call came in from Uncle Vito.

The second part of his plan was to contact Boris Segura, to let him know that Creshanko would have the seven eggs at one location, his home.   Carter had promised Boris he would let him know when Creshanko had all seven eggs if indeed he had found them. The secret of the diamond egg would remain with Carter until he saw fit to disclose it.

While at the bank, Carter decided to rent a second safe deposit box to temporarily store the satchel and then went to his office. Waiting at the office when he arrived was Det. Croft, who asked him, "Where the hell have you been, Carter?"

"On a scavenger hunt, Croft."

"You know Carter that Volasko woman we're holding kept insisting that she never shot that Russian, or anyone else. The blood on the gun was the Russian's, but the bullets didn't match according to ballistics."

"So are you going to turn her loose, Croft?"

"Hell no. Somehow she's involved with those other homicides and I'm holding her as long as I can. Another thing Carter, she says if you don't get her a good lawyer, she's going to scramble some eggs. Now what the hell did she mean by that?"

"She probably wants to cut my balls off Croft, and smash them with a hammer."

"Well her fingerprints are all over that room at the Sportsmen Lodge, and right now she's my only suspect for the killing. But without the gun or some other proof, she could be back on the street in forty-eight hours."

"Croft I'll make a deal with you, you keep her ass cooling in jail for another forty-eight hours, and I think I'll be able to clear up those other homicides for you."

"Carter if you're holding back evidence, I swear, I'll have *your* ass cooling in a cell."

"Trust me Croft, forty-eight hours, what have you got to lose?"

"Not much, just my fucking pension, Carter, if this plan of yours backfires. You screw me around on this and I'll fry your ass."

"Have I ever let you down Croft?"

"I don't have enough fingers to count that high Carter."

"Trust me Croft, and you'll be able to tie up all those homicides and clear the books."

After a few seconds of silence, the detective said, "Okay you got two days, don't fuck up Carter. I'll have your ass sitting in one of the back cells where you might be forgotten about. By the way, what's that Russian's connection to all of this?"

"In time Croft, don't push it. I'll tell this, he's in it up to his ass."

"Yeah, and right now so are you. If I don't hear from you real soon, I'll be knocking on your door."

26

Carter spent most of the afternoon straightening and cleaning the office after the hectic week. A couple calls came in from prospective customers and he just let the answering machine handle them. Then around 6:30 as he was getting ready to leave, the call he was waiting for, "Mr. Carter, Vito Terratello here, how are you this evening?"

"Hello Mr. Terratello, I'm fine thank you."

"Please, call me Vito."

"Thank you Vito and you must call me Don."

"Don, is that short for Donald?"

"Yes it is, although I can't get your nephew to stop calling me Donny Boy."

After a slight laugh, "Donald it is. I'm calling to let you know that I'll be flying out to California in the morning. I was hoping that you and my nephew might be able to meet me at the airport when I get in. If possible we could have an early lunch together before I have to make my meeting in Los Angeles in the afternoon?"

"I would be honored Vito. Please let me know what flight you'll be on and the time of arrival and we'll be there. So I guess that antique dealer I put you in touch with worked out in a positive way?"

Vito paused a little, "Yes Donald, he was very cooperative. Thank you."

The conversation ended after Vito gave arrival information and he told Carter he was looking forward to meeting him. Carter then called Mick and told him about the plans for the following day.

The next conversation was with Serge Creshanko, informing him that the following afternoon he could pick up his precious eggs at his office around 5PM.

The third call was to Boris Segura who was actually in Washington D.C., but returned the call in fifteen minutes after getting the message from his answering service.

Boris informed Carter that he would be in California the following day for a meeting with an old friend and would call after he arrived in town.

Carter asked, "Boris, is this a secured line?"

"Yes it is Mr. Carter, is yours?"

"Yes sir, I had it checked today."

"Fine, then we can say whatever we wish in confidence of privacy."

"Well Boris, I wanted you to know that I located those eggs and I have them in my possession."

"That is wonderful news Mr. Carter. I will pay you handsomely when I arrive in town tomorrow."

"I would like nothing better than to turn them over to you Boris, but I have to fulfill my obligation to my client."

"Mr. Carter, what about *our* agreement?"

"I have a plan that will benefit both of us and I'm sure it is one that you will appreciate, but it may involve some of your old homeland skills."

"Perhaps Mr. Carter, we should wait until we are face to face to discus the particulars of your plan."

"I also think that's a good idea Boris. We can finish this conversation tomorrow. I'll be waiting for your call."

Feeling like a lot of the pieces of the puzzle were coming together, Carter decided to call it a night and head on home.

The following morning, Carter was enjoying a cup of coffee in his kitchen and reading the daily newspaper when he heard the front doorbell ring. It was 8am and Mick was standing on the front steps smiling, "Rise and shine, we need to get to the airport ASAP."

"Mick, your uncle isn't due to land for another three hours."

"Change of plans Donny Boy. Uncle Vito decided to hire a private jet and he lands in one hour."

"Oh shit! I better get my ass moving then. Have some coffee Mick while I get dressed. Do you know where to pick him up?"

"All arranged Donny Boy, we drive the limo to the security gate and......"

Carter asked, "Limo, what limo?"

"The one I have parked outside. Come on, get going, our chauffeur is waiting."

The drive to Burbank Airport took only a half hour, but getting through security took another fifteen minutes. Parking off to the side, they waited another fifteen minutes and watched as the corporate jet slowly pulled up in front of a private hangar and shut down its engine. As the side door opened and the steps lowered, the chauffeur pulled the limo closer to the plane.

A large man in a black suit about thirty was the first to deplane and as he stopped on the top step, he looked in all directions and then leaned his head back into the plane. He next continued down the steps and waited for his boss to exit.

The next man out of the door was a well dressed man about sixty years old who was obviously Vito Terratello, easily recognizable by his demeanor. When he saw Mick, a wide smile appeared on his face as he walked towards the limo and Mick met him halfway.

Vito hugged his nephew and said, "Michael, it is so good to see you again, your mother sends her love and wishes you to call her soon. You know Michael, family is very important. One should never forget his roots."

Looking at Carter, Vito said, "And this must be Donald, am I correct?"

Carter offered his hand and the two men shook, with Vito saying, "I am pleased to meet the friend Michael talks so highly about."

"And Vito, I am so pleased to meet you. I want to thank you for your favors to me."

Mick said, "Okay, enough talk for now."

Vito and Carter looked at Mick and laughed.

Vito said, "I have made reservations for brunch at the hotel I am staying at, and I would like you both to join me. It is at the Beverly Hilton Hotel."

Carter said, "We know it well Vito."

Vito asked, "Michael, have you discussed any of what we talked about with Donald?"

"No Uncle I have not."

Vito looked at Carter, "Please trust me Donald. It is better that we all discuss it later."

27

Vito's suite at the Beverly Hilton was as large as Carter's house and his office all thrown in for good measure. After dropping off the luggage and a few minutes of freshening up, the men were ready for brunch.

Vito, Mick and Carter enjoyed a wonderful meal and exhilarating conversation, which included many questions Vito had about the past couple weeks. Carter held nothing back yet felt the wise old man knew much more than he let on. Once they finished their meal they all returned to Vito's suite where his associate, Gino, was watching over a special package for Carter.

During their conversation, Vito did reveal much information about Serge Creshanko that he passed on to Carter. He told him, "Donald, be very careful with this man Creshanko, he has no feelings about human life. I would call him a pig, but that would do a discredit to all the pigs of the world. In my brief dealing with him a couple of years ago, I came very close to exterminating that piece of crap and doing the world a service. The money you had requested from him was delivered to me by a special messenger. I spoke with him and requested that it be done in that way. I had no desire to look at that man's face ever again."

Turning to his nephew, Vito put a hand on his shoulder, "Michael, you also must be very careful. Explaining your death to your mother would tear my heart out."

Mick told him, "Uncle, all will be fine and I promise we will both be very careful."

"Donald, please excuse the whims of an old man. I need to have a few words with Michael in private. I promise we will not be very long."

"Of course Vito, I'll just wait outside on the patio."

"Donald, before you leave today, I have a special package for you. I thank you for your gift, and I promise I will put it to good use."

"And I thank you for your help collecting my fee from Serge Creshanko."

The two men hugged and Carter said, "I look forward to dinner tomorrow night Vito." Then he left the room.

About fifteen minutes went by before Mick came out followed by Gino carrying a neatly wrapped package.

The package, which Carter knew contained one hundred thousand dollars, was quite small in size, but it put a big smile on his face.

Carter and Mick left the hotel and headed first to the Bank of America. As Mick drove, Carter tore open one corner of the package, smiled and said, "This must have really pissed off that Russian bastard." Then he asked, "Mick, what is it that you and Vito don't want me to know yet?"

"Donny Boy, you know I love you like a brother. But please, I can not betray my Uncle's trust. You'll just have to wait. I don't know all of it yet myself, so I guess we'll both find out at the same time."

They needed to pick up the satchel and drop off the money in the safe deposit box. The cash in the bag and the jewelry had been taken out and would also be left behind in the bank deposit box.

Carter's plan was to give the satchel to Creshanko, while Mick sat in the office with a 9mm resting in his lap.

During the drive to the office, Mick told Carter, "Donny Boy, Uncle Vito told me a few things that he *does* want me to reveal to you. He understands your legal obligation to complete your contract with Creshanko. There is much more that we talked about, as I told you before, that I can *not* tell you. Out of respect to you, he didn't want me to have to lie to you. He said after your dealing with Creshanko has been completed, he has some personal issues he must settle with that pig. I don't know what the issues are, but I think it's better for us not to know."

"Mick, I understand, as far as I'm concerned, I never heard any part of that explanation. But thank you."

Arriving at his office, Carter was surprised to see Creshanko's limo parked in the lot. Also Annie's car was parked near the steps. It was only 3pm, two hours early for their scheduled 5pm meeting, and Carter had a bad feeling.

When Carter and Mick walked into the office, Creshanko was seated in Carter's chair with his feet up on the desk as he greeted him, "Hello Mr. Carter, is that by chance my property in the bag you're carrying?"

"Get your damn feet off of my desk Creshanko." Looking around but not seeing Annie, Carter said, "Where the hell is my secretary?"

Slowly putting his feet down on the floor, Creshanko said, "That pretty young secretary of yours is just fine Mr. Carter, she is in the company of one of my associates. When we have finished our business she will be released unharmed."

Mick had removed his 9mm from his waistband and walked over to a chair in the corner and sat down. He placed his weapon on his lap and smiled at the Russian.

Creshanko laughed as he moved to the couch and said, "Do you think that will help to get the girl back?"

Carter placed the satchel on the desk and took out the towel covering the eggs. Taking out one of the eggs and un-wrapping it, he then held it up for Creshanko to see. Carter then asked Mick, "Hey Mick, open the window would you please?"

Creshanko laughed and said, "You want me to believe you would do something so foolish?"

Carter took out the other two eggs and un-wrapped them laying them on the towel and said, "Creshanko, I don't give a shit what you believe, but when I count to three I'm tossing one of these eggs out the window. When I get to six another one goes out and the last one at nine. I got my money already, these things don't mean shit to me. Get my secretary back here now."

Creshanko just laughed, and Carter said, "ONE", carrying an egg as he walked to the window."

Creshanko said, "Mr. Carter be sensible."

Carter said, "TWO", and lifted his hand in a throwing motion.

Creshanko stood and said, "Wait Mr. Carter, I will call Alex to bring your girl back. No need to do anything foolish."

Carter walked slowly back and stood next to his desk and watched Creshanko.

"May I use your phone, Mr. Carter?"

"Make your call."

Creshanko used the phone on the desk and called his associate on the limo car phone and instructed him in Russian to return with the girl.

Carter told him, "If she is even scratched Creshanko, I will cut a piece out of your ass."

After placing the receiver back in its cradle, Creshanko picked up one of the eggs and said, "Have you ever seen anything this beautiful before Mr. Carter?"

"Like I said before Creshanko, they ain't shit to me. As far as I'm concerned now, they could have just dropped out of a chicken's ass."

A few minutes went by when they heard footsteps coming up the metal stairs. Annie Dugan was the first one to walk in the door followed by another one of Creshanko's big gorillas in a black suit.

Carter asked, "Are you okay sweetheart?"

"Yeah I'm fine Mr. Carter, he never touched me, just scared the hell out of me. I'm so sorry. I know you told me to stay home, but I needed to get a few things from my desk. When I walked in they were already here."

"Its okay sweetheart, everything will be fine from now on. Why don't you go to your desk and check on some of the messages on the machine."

Carter looked at Creshanko, "Take your goddamn eggs and get the hell out of here you Russian bastard. I've delivered and you've paid. Our business is over and done, you are no longer my client. You come around here again and I'll shoot you on sight."

Placing all the wrapped eggs in the satchel, Creshanko said, "Very true, Mr. Carter, you completed your part of the bargain, but we *will* meet again, that I promise." And then he left.

Mick looked at Carter and said, "That's a man who could use one right between the eyes, and I'd love to be the one to deliver it."

"Mick, hopefully our dealings with him are over, but now the next step is to turn over the diamond egg to that Boris character tonight, as soon as he shows up."

"When's that Donny Boy?"

"Well he's supposed to be here in a few hours, I'm waiting for his call."

"Annie Dugan who was standing in the doorway asked, "Diamond egg, what is a diamond egg?"

Carter said with a smile, "It's one a chicken didn't lay sweetheart, it's a long story."

The phone rang and Annie hustled to the front office to answer it. A few seconds passed and Annie came back and said, "Mr. Carter, it's that man who says his name is Boris."

"Perfect Annie, I'll take it."

Answering the phone, Carter said, "Hello Boris, I was just thinking about you."

"Wonderful Mr. Carter, everything has gone as planned I hope?"

"Yes Boris, Creshanko left my office only fifteen minutes ago with the three eggs."

Surprisingly Boris asked, "And what about the fourth egg Mr. Carter, do you still have it in your possession?"

Completely caught off guard, Carter asked, "Boris, how do you know about the fourth egg?"

"Mr. Carter, there are many things that I know, some of which will be much clearer to you in a few days. I hope you were wise enough to determine the proper egg to hold back to your possession?"

"You mean the one with the diamond in its belly?"

Laughing, Boris said, "Ah, the diamond."

"Boris, will you be coming here this afternoon?"

"There is no need now Mr. Carter, but we will see each other in the very near future. Keep the remaining egg in a safe place until you have been asked to transport it. I will be calling you. Goodbye Mr. Carter."

Hanging up the phone, Carter appeared to be completely confused and told Mick, "How the hell did he find out about the fourth egg?"

"Don't look at me, Donny Boy."

Carter said, "There's only one other person who knows there were four eggs." They both said at the same time, "Reggie."

Carter called out to Annie, "Sweetheart, would you see if you can get Det. Croft on the phone for me?"

A couple minutes passed and Annie called out, "Det. Croft is on line one Mr. Carter."

Picking up the phone, Carter said, "Hello Croft, how are you?"

"How am I? I'm pissed off, how are you? Your damn bimbo made bail Carter. Some polished ass, high class lawyer got a judge to issue a release, so she's back on the street. So you tell me, how should I be? My only suspect that I can tie to three homicides walks. I swear there ain't no justice in this world. So what the hell do you really want

Carter? I hope you have something for me to brighten my fucking day?"

"Well Croft, you told me what I wanted to know in a round about way."

"Carter, answer me damn it, you got something you're not telling me?"

"Not yet Croft, but when I do, I'll be calling you. I still have another twenty-four hours."

Hanging up the phone, Carter said, "She made bail. Reggie made bail with the help of some high class lawyer. Does this have something to do with what you can't tell me Mick?"

"You're putting me on a spot Donny Boy. I have no idea how in hell she know this Boris guy. Please, you need to wait and talk with Vito."

"Damned if I know Mick. We'll just have to wait and see how it plays out."

"Well, I guess it's a good time for me to call my uncle. He wants us to meet him for dinner tomorrow night if everything plays out the way it's supposed to. He asked me to call when you were finished with Creshanko."

Carter said, "What the hell. Give him a call. Tell him the Russian is no longer a client."

A quick call to Vito, then Mick was off the phone. "Uncle Vito sends his regards. He wants us to meet him tomorrow night for dinner at the hotel at 8PM if that's alright with you. Also he said to bring the egg with you."

"Here we go again Mick. How does Vito know that there were four eggs? Are you sure you didn't let it slip?"

"No, I'm sure."

"Sounds good, eight o'clock will be fine. I'm looking forward to putting an end to it all."

"Hey Donny Boy, what do you think about you, me and Annie going over to Rusty's for a little celebration?"

"You two go Mick, I'm heading home."

28

Awakening around 9am, after a full eight hours of sleep and feeling like the weight of the world had been lifted from his shoulders was something new for Carter.

After a complete breakfast that he prepared for himself, Carter called Annie at the office and told her he would be in by eleven. With a smile on his face and a good feeling in his wallet, even the drive on the freeway to North Hollywood was a pleasure.

Walking into the office after stopping at the bank to pick up the last egg and a bit of cash, Carter noticed Annie had purchased a small bouquet of daisies and placed them in a glass of water on her desk. Counting out one thousand dollars in hundred dollar bills, Carter said, "Your bonus Sweetheart."

After pointing at the flowers and saying, "Nice touch Annie," Carter went into his office and sat at his desk. A few minutes went by and Annie came in with her notebook and told him they may have a couple of new customers. The day just seemed to continue in that direction until it was time for Annie to go to the bank then home.

At 4:45 Annie walked into Carter's office and told him, "I'm going to take off early and stop at the Post Office to mail some overdue payments before I go to the bank, Mr. C.

Carter said, "That's fine Annie. Do you realize this is the first day in a long while that we didn't get even one call from Creshanko, Croft, Boris, or even Mick? Don't get me wrong, I love Mick like a brother. By the way, how was your date last night with Mickey T?"

"Mr. Carter, you wouldn't want me to kiss and tell, would you?"

"No Sweetheart, don't worry, I'll get the poop from Mick. Have a good night and I'll see you tomorrow."

Around 5:30PM, Carter decided to stop for the day. He turned on the phone answering machine, locked up the office, and headed down the steps.

IT must have been right around the time he was driving out of the gate when the answering machine was recording a phone call from Det. Croft. *"Carter, this is Det. Croft. I need you to call me ASAP. Do you hear me Carter? You have a lot of explaining to do. I have a few more homicides on my hands and I know you're mixed up in this somehow. You need to get your ass in here now Carter."* The message would not be heard until the next morning, because Carter had a dinner appointment at eight and he would not be coming back to the office that night.

A private dining room had been set up for Vito Terratello and his guests at the Beverly Hilton for a special dinner party. After being led to the dining room by one of Vito's associates, while he carried a plain paper bag containing the priceless egg, Carter was surprised to see Mick already there sitting and joking with his Uncle. Another man seated with his back towards Carter stood up, turned and greeted him by saying, "Hello again Mr. Carter, so nice to once again have the pleasure of your company.

Carter was speechless, but managed to get out, "Good evening Boris, it's nice to see you again also."

Vito motioned to a chair, "Please have a seat, Donald."

Sitting down still in a state of total surprise, Carter said, "Vito, I'm sorry, I had no idea you and Boris were acquainted."

Vito smiled and put his hand on Boris' shoulder, "Boris and I have known each other for many years Donald, and I hope for many more to follow."

Carter looked at Mick and asked, "You knew about this Mick?"

Sitting back in his chair, Mick said, "Just found out about this tonight Donny Boy."

Vito laughed and said, "Michael, you refer to Donald as Donny Boy, why is that?"

Before Mick could start to speak, Boris asked, "May I Michael?"

After a small head nod by Mick, Boris went on. "Many years ago, while Michael, Donald, and another man named Daniel McKay were stationed at Fort Hood, Texas, the three men became very good friends. They were like the Three Musketeers from what I've heard. Am I correct so far Mr. Carter?"

In complete amazement, Carter asked, "How do you know this Boris?"

"It's what I do Mr. Carter." Continuing, Boris said, "The men all had buddy names for each other. At one point they were all separated by duty assignments but later re-united."

Before Boris could go on, a knock was heard at the door and a few seconds later another person was escorted into the room and all the men stood up as Vito said, "Good evening Miss Volasko."

This time Carter had a question, "Would someone explain what is going on here, because I'm very confused."

Vito said, "Donald, as the evening goes on, I promise all will be explained."

As Boris went on with his story about the three musketeers, Reggie Volasko took her seat next to Vito. Boris said, "Donald Carter, who was called 'Donny Boy,' went on to join the police force in Los Angeles. Michael Terratello, who was known as 'Mickey T.,' worked in security in New York. Dan McKay, known as 'Irish Dan,' stayed in the military and wound up staying in Vietnam several years after resigning his commission."

Carter just listened in amazement at all that Boris was revealing.

Another knock came at the door and one of Vito's associates checked to see who it was. The man said, "Mr. Terratello, dinner is ready to be served. Should I let them in?"

Vito addressed all at the table, "My guests. Let us enjoy our meals and we can talk after. Show them in Bruno."

Dinner was over and Carter had respected Vito's wishes not asking questions during the meal, but was constantly staring down Reggie. The spumoni and anisette were being served by the waiter, when Carter started to ask a question. Vito held a finger to his lip and then motioned for Bruno to have the waiter leave and to lock the door behind them.

Vito turned to Carter and said, "Donald, Boris and I have known each other for over twenty years. My old friend contacted me last month and informed me of a sting operation he had in mind to take down Serge Creshanko. That man meant nothing to me until Boris informed me that I too would like to see Creshanko suffer. I had no idea what he was talking about until he explained. Through small business dealings that I had with Creshanko I remembered that I didn't like the man but I couldn't care much if he lived or died.

My sister Angela's son, Anthony DeMarco, another one of my nephews, was killed years ago in Milan, Italy. Anthony worked as a courier for a private museum in Milan. Along with his duties of cleaning and restoring old antiques, Anthony also drove a delivery truck for the museum. It was on one of these pick ups, that he was stopped by robbers who killed him and stole the antiques in the truck. Along with several paintings that were worth in excess of one hundred thousand dollars, a Fabergé Egg was also stolen. None of the items were ever recovered, but through the help of Boris,

I found out that Creshanko was the one who ordered the death of my nephew in the robbery."

Carter asked, "Vito, may I ask why such an elaborate scheme to get Creshanko?"

Boris spoke up and said, "May I Vito?

Vito gave a slight nod and Boris said, "Mr. Carter, I asked Vito for a favor to help me retrieve the Fabergé Eggs for my country, and in turn we would both have the pleasure of destroying that piece of vermin."

Carter asked, "But Boris, how did Dan McKay, Reggie Volasko and I fit into all of this? Why were we brought in at all?"

Boris said, "We needed to be sure Creshanko would take his four eggs out of hiding to display them. We knew he would do this once he got the remaining three from you after you located them. In the world he belonged to it was known that the four Fabergé Eggs he possessed were well hidden, but his ego and power were things he pushed in people's faces. He spread the word around town that he would have all the eggs in one place for the first time in forty years. He was preparing to invite a select group and display his prize possessions. Once he paid out the money to Vito two days ago, he let it be known that he owned them all."

Carter said, "But what good does it do us now Boris?" He does have them all and they are worth a fortune and he has the last laugh on everyone."

Boris looked at Vito as he said, "Mr. Carter, did you bring the remaining egg with you as you were asked?"

Carter got up from the table and walked over to where his overcoat was hanging and retrieved a paper bag and brought it back to the table.

Boris asked, "Is this the one that the water faded the star?"

"How did you know that?" Carter asked.

Boris said, "Would you please remove it from the bag Mr. Carter?"

Carefully removing the valuable egg from the bag, Carter handed it to Boris.

Taking his napkin and dipping it in his water glass, Boris then dabbed the seventh star on the egg and watched it disappear and reappear, and then he smiled. Wrapping the egg in his cloth napkin, Boris then said something in Russian to his associate who now stood by the door. The man took the egg from him and walked to the corner of the room. Placing the egg on the thick tiled floor the man picked up a hammer that had been placed near the corner and smashed the egg.

Carter said, "What are you doing, that's the egg with the diamond in it."

Boris reassured him, "No Mr. Carter, it is not."

Carter said, "But the instructions said….."

Boris cut in and said, "The instructions were written by me Mr. Carter, it was part of the sting. That egg contains a piece of glass and is a phony copy of another yet to be located egg."

From under the table, Boris lifted the blue TWA satchel and placed it on the table in front of Carter and asked, "Do you recognize this Mr. Carter?"

"Yes, it's the satchel I gave to Creshanko, but how did you get it?"

Vito now spoke up, "That is something you do not want to know Donald."

Opening the satchel, Boris spread out all seven eggs on the table and said, "You'll notice a small red dot on the bottom of one egg, please separate that one from the rest and do the same water test on it."

Doing what he was told, Carter saw the same results as the phony. Looking at Boris, Carter asked, "That means that there are two phony copies but it wasn't one of the eggs I gave him?"

"Exactly Mr. Carter, the real egg with the diamond in it is still out there somewhere unknown."

Carter asked, "And Creshanko, he didn't know?"

Boris said, "Do not trouble yourself with Creshanko, he will never trouble anyone again."

Vito spoke, "I think that's quite enough my friend. We do not want to place Donald in a position that would not fit his morals."

Carter asked, "Boris, what about Miss Volasko? Why was she such a big part of the sting?"

Vito answered, "Donald, Miss Volasko worked for me and was a very important part of the plan and came on board after she found out about the death of her brother-in-law, Dan McKay."

"What about the charges she is facing with the police and her involvement in a few homicides?"

Vito answered, "All the charges will be dropped against Miss Volasko within a couple days Donald. I assure you that."

Reggie spoke up for the first time and said, "I'm sorry Carter, as you can see now, I couldn't tell you anything of what was going on."

Carter asked, "And the Fabergé Eggs, Boris, what will you do with them?"

"The seven eggs will be returned to my country and placed in the museum with the other ones that have been located. There are still many of the original eggs unaccounted for. Maybe someday, the Fabergé Egg with the diamond in it will surface again. For now Mr. Carter, my people will think that we have the real thing back in our homeland. That will help to give us back a little pride in Mother Russia. I want to thank you all for your help."

Carter asked, "Boris what about the jewels and money we found in the satchel?

Laughing, Boris said, "The jewelry, I'm sorry to say is all glass and paste, I don't think one piece in the pile is worth over five dollars."

"What about the money Boris, there was twenty thousand in the bottom of the satchel under the eggs?"

Boris laughed again and said, "Mr. Carter, that money was supposed to be your finder's fee. I was very happy to find out that you made other arrangements and extracted two hundred thousand dollars from Creshanko. So nothing has changed, that money is still yours my friend for a job well done."

Vito said with a smile. "And Donald, the one hundred thousand you had me keep from Creshanko, I am giving to Michael and Miss Volasko to split between them."

Mick spoke up and said, "Thank you Uncle Vito."

Reggie also spoke up, "Thank you very much Mr. Terratello. That is most kind of you."

Vito said, "Miss Volasko, I am so sorry for your loss of family members, I only hope the money will help comfort you even in some small way. Your sister and her friends in Palmdale were innocent people tortured by Creshanko and the vicious people who worked for him."

Vito then said, "Now, if there are no more questions, let us enjoy the spumoni and toast to the last we have to hear of Serge Creshanko."

As they all raised their glasses, Cater remained staring at Reggie, and said, "We need to talk Reggie, we have things that need to be worked out between us."

"In time Carter, but that time is not now."

29

Forty-eight hours had gone by since the dinner party at the Beverly Hilton. Reggie had still not spoken to Carter other than her telling him that night, "Just stay away from me Carter. I have to leave for a couple of days and assist Mr. Terratello in San Francisco. We'll talk when I get back."

Reggie had left on a flight out of town a couple hours after the party broke up with Vito. She was handling some private business for Vito with a group of San Francisco investors.

Two days later, Carter was locking up his office door with plans of meeting Mick at Rusty's Hacienda. As he walked to the outside steps he saw Reggie standing there, "Do you have a little time to talk Carter?"

"What the hell do you want Reggie? I tried to talk with you the other night and you brushed me off, so now *you* have time for me?"

"Business with Mr. Terratello had to come first Carter. I also wanted the dust to settle before we tried to smoke the peace pipe. I needed to get past everything that happened to me also."

"Oh, so now you're ready to talk and I'm supposed to give you your stage, is that it?"

"Carter. Why are you being such an ass? You had me locked up remember. You called that asshole detective and he threw my ass in jail. Now, can we talk or should I just go on my way?"

Carter stayed silent for about ten seconds staring at her, and then asked, "Can you cook?"

"Can I cook?"

"Food, can you cook food?"

"Get me into a kitchen and I'll cook a meal like a gourmet chef. What did you have in mind?"

"We'll see Reggie. Come on, let's go food shopping."

"So, I cook you dinner and that's how I get you to talk with me?"

"It's a start Reggie."

"And how do we finish Carter?"

Carter smiled and said, "Hopefully at the same time, all sweaty and exhausted."

"Very funny Carter, very funny. So where are we going food shopping?"

Carter called Mick at Rusty's Hacienda on his car phone and told him something came up and he couldn't meet him. When Mick asked, "Yeah, what's her name Donny Boy?"

Carter laughed and said, "Patricia Wade. See you tomorrow Mick."

Carter and Reggie did their food shopping at Gelson's Market on Riverside Drive, in North Hollywood, then drove to Carter's house in Chatsworth. They carried the bags of groceries into the house, put a few things away in the refrigerator and left the rest unpacked on the counter.

Reggie had no intentions of having sex with Carter, but sometimes the energy, emotions and attraction for each other can start a fire burning that just gets out of control. They say that opposites attract, but in this case these were two people who were so much alike it was spooky. So dinner plans were put on hold for the next two hours until they finished with some apology sex for appetizers.

Afterwards, Reggie cooked a great dinner just like she promised, then they talked for awhile and then it was back to the bedroom where they had some wonderful intense sex for dessert. And like Carter had said earlier, they got all sweaty and exhausted and finished up simultaneously. It seemed all was forgiven, but time would tell.

The next morning while taking a shower together, they had some shower sex and then finally had breakfast.

Around 10AM Carter and Reggie drove to the office and found Det. Croft waiting seated behind Carter's desk. Annie told Carter as soon as he walked in the door that the detective was in his office and had been there about twenty minutes.

Det. Croft greeted the couple by saying, "Well good morning you two love birds, just return from your honeymoon?"

Carter said, "Croft, first off, get the hell out of my chair. Second, I've had just about enough of your bullshit, tell me what's on that dumb-ass mind of yours or get the hell out of my office."

Walking over to the couch Croft said, "Fine Carter, no bullshit. First, your little sweetheart there has had all the charges dropped against her. New evidence has come up that completely exonerates Miss Volasko of any crimes she had been charged with. Second, Carter, what was your actual involvement with Serge Creshanko?"

"He was a client, but we concluded our business a few days ago. Why?"

"Did your business dealings end on a high note, or did you have a falling out?"

"Get to it Croft, or get the hell out."

"Mr. Creshanko was found by his maid yesterday morning in a very unresponsive mood.

He was sitting on a couch in his den and when she tried talking to him he was not receptive to her questions. It seems he had a hard time talking because of the two bullet holes in his head. He was accompanied by two yet to be identified men who also were quite dead. An automatic weapon that ballistics' matched to the killing of the stiff found at Sportsmen's Lodge was used to kill one of the men at Creshanko's little party. Another weapon that had been used to kill Victor Yeltsin, whose body was found in the L.A. River, was also recovered at the house. It looked at first to be a robbery gone bad, but very little appeared to be missing according to the maid. A large glass display case that the maid said contained some jewel figurines and decorated eggs was the only thing destroyed with some of the contents scattered around the room. There were two armed guards who were also found dead on the property outside."

Carter interrupted and asked, "What the hell does this all have to do with me, Croft? Do you have a good reason for telling me all this shit?"

"Well I'll tell you Carter, I think you and your little lady there are mixed up in this right up to your asses. When I find that connection, I'll be back here with a warrant for both of you. So for now you can go back to playing house and whatever it is that you have on your minds."

You know what, Croft, until that day comes, how about you just stay the hell away from me. For someone who just closed a few homicides, you don't seem too happy, 'Detective Stanley Croft.' Now please, get the hell out of my office, I have work to do."

As Det. Croft left, Carter called out to Annie, "Sweetheart. What do we have on the books for today?"

30

Several months had gone by since Boris reunited the Fabergé Eggs with the others on display at the museum in Russia. He was very thankful to Carter for his hard work and even sent a formal invitation to his new friend to view the display as his guest.

In a little town on the outskirts of the industrialized city of Ekaterinburg, located in the Ural Mountains eight-hundred miles east of St. Petersburg, Russia, a little girl was asking the new priest of their church, "Father, do the old things on the shelf in the rectory have any meaning to our town history?"

The priest, whose name was Father Misov Bochefski, said with a smile, "Anna, the silver plate, golden chalice and jewel covered egg were all gifts to the church by the Czar Nicholas II of the Romanov family only weeks before the execution of his entire family back in 1918."

Anna asked, "Because they are so old, are they very valuable, Father Misov?"

"Sometimes my child, the value has nothing to do with money, but instead the thought and love behind the giving. I believe they were given to the church for safe keeping so that one day the gift will help us to build a larger parish so we can pass on the word of the Lord to many more people."

"Will the church try to sell them some day Father?"

Father Misov said with a smile, "Maybe some day my child, but for now they will remain in the safety of the church where they can be admired for what they are."

"With all their jewels aren't you worried about someone stealing them Father?"

"I don't believe anyone would expect to find something of great value in a poor parish like ours my child."

THE END